my heart wants

the heart duet

NICOLE S. GOODIN

My Heart Wants
Published by Nicole S. Goodin
ISBN: 978-0-473-44917-9
Copyright 2018 by Nicole S. Goodin
All rights reserved. ©

Cover design by Nicole Goodin
Images purchased from Deposit Photos
Editing by Spell Bound

For Ruby

"She believed she could, so she did."
-Author unknown

There have been plenty of times when I've felt nervous in my life. I can think of half a dozen that spring to mind in an instant, and they're all to do with my heart.

This is too, but not in the same way.

This is something new.

This is about what my heart wants, not what it needs for once, and all that my heart wants in this moment, is him.

Prologue

Rylan
2015

I don't know what I'm doing back at this window; this is the third time I've stood in this spot in the last hour alone.

I know I should do something, *anything* other than just linger here... but I don't know how to break away.

There's *something* keeping me here right now, and in a world where nothing seems to make sense anymore, I *need* this feeling, if only to get through the next few minutes.

I glance back at the girl in the bed.

If I had to guess, I'd say she was about nineteen years old – far too young to look the way she does.

She's pale and gaunt and if I hadn't had to witness first-hand my sister's life in this world coming to an end, I would have sworn that nobody had ever looked as close to death as the girl behind this small glass window.

She's motionless. So, *so* still and I worry for a moment that she's dead too.

The only thing reassuring me she's still alive, even though it's really no business of mine, is the continuous beep from the monitor next to her, making it clear that her heart is, in fact, still beating – that it's doing the very thing that my sister's isn't.

A loud sob rips through my body at the thought.

Doctors and nurses move around the hall but none of them bother me; most of them avoid eye contact entirely.

They know why I'm still aimlessly wandering the halls of the intensive care unit.

My sister may have had no brain function for a couple of days, but now she's officially gone. The machines aren't breathing for her anymore – there's nothing left keeping her alive.

I don't know what to do, I've never felt this alone or unsure in my entire life.

I know I need to leave; I need to be anywhere that's not inside these hospital walls, but I can't seem to make that happen.

I know I can't stay here forever, but I'm terrified that walking out the door will make everything even more real than it already is.

I'm not sure who I'm trying to fool with my logic – this couldn't possibly be any more real, and deep down I know that it's not going to make a difference if I stay or go.

She's gone.

I take one more look at the girl and promise myself that this will be the last time I'll ever see her.

I allow my eyes to linger on her motionless form, and as I finally find the will to turn around, her arm moves, and my breath catches in my throat.

I watch her as though she's some type of miracle, and maybe she is, as she slowly wakes and eventually glances over at the sleeping figure in the chair next to her.

I see the side of her face curve and I know she's smiling.

Her head rolls slightly in my direction and the wave of pain that crosses her features is so sudden and intense that I rush forward a step.

She catches my movement out of the corner of her eye, and I stop dead in my tracks.

The nurse from the corner is rushing towards her, but she doesn't look away from me.

All I really see are her eyes – surrounded by dark circles, they are the most beautiful crystal blue eyes I've ever seen. Even filled with pain, and dulled with obvious sickness, I've never seen anything like them.

She stares at me – a total stranger, and I stare back at her, with one lone tear rolling down my cheek.

Three years later

Chapter One

Violet

"What if this guy's a sociopath, huh? What happens then?" I demand.

"Calm down, I've heard he's *really* nice."

"Oh 'you've heard' have you? He could be a killer just waiting for the right opportunity for all you know."

Lucy pauses from applying the makeup to my face and rolls her eyes.

"You watch way too much C.S.I."

I huff out a breath. "You're not wrong, but that's not the point... what if he's a murder rapist, hmmm? You want that on your conscience?"

"Stop being such a drama queen and show me what you think you're going to wear."

"What do you mean, what I *think* I'm going to wear? I'm perfectly capable of putting clothes on my body, thank you very much."

I know as well as she does that she's just successfully distracted me from my irrational fears, but for now at least, I've got bigger fish to fry.

"Baggy t-shirts and jeans don't count as clothes, Letty."

"I wasn't going to wear a t-shirt," I grumble as I slide off the chair.

I pull out a long-sleeve blouse and a pair of black pants from my closet and wave them at her.

She screws up her nose in a look of distaste. "It's a date, not a funeral."

She might only be joking, but I've worn that exact outfit to a funeral before, so she actually has a point.

I shoot her daggers anyway as I rummage through the closet again, this time emerging with a denim skirt and a green knit, high-neck jumper.

"Oh, good God no... *not* the snot colour jersey."

I throw the clothes onto the chair in the corner and groan in frustration. "You find me something then."

We both know she's going to get her way in the long run anyway – she always does.

"I'll do you one better." She grins wickedly, and I seriously fear for myself in this moment.

I may have survived more operations and treatments than I can count, but Lucy's hare-brained schemes still scare the life out of me like nothing else.

Her and her ideas are the reason I'm preparing for a blind date right now.

Her husband, Emmett, is no better than she is. The guy I've been forced into meeting tonight is someone he knows from work apparently – so he's as much to blame for this mess as she is.

"You know, I would have thought that being seven months pregnant would have slowed you down, even just a little bit."

She turns and sticks her tongue out at me over her shoulder. "Not a chance."

She pulls out a shopping bag, and I'm instantly nervous at the sight of it.

Lucy is always pointing items out on clothing racks at stores and telling me how good things would look on me.

She's sweet, and if it wasn't for the big scar that runs down the centre of my chest, she'd be absolutely right.

If it wasn't for the marks on my skin, I probably would have tried on the plunging-neckline dress she'd pointed out to me two weeks ago.

But that's not me. I'm scarred, I'm flawed. And I'm okay with keeping those parts of myself hidden. Lucy, however, doesn't seem to see my scars when she looks at me, and while that's a blessing in itself, right now, it has the potential to be a curse.

She waddles over with the bag and holds it out to me.

I reach for it as though it's a bomb that could go off at any minute, because, quite frankly, it is.

"It won't bite." She laughs as she shoves it into my waiting hands. "Oh, ye of little faith."

"Does it have sequins?" I wince.

"Nope."

"Glitter?"

"Nope again."

She sits herself down in the chair I sat in while she painted my face on.

"Plunging neckline?"

I brace myself for the answer.

"Just open the bag, Violet."

I peek inside and am greeted by the sight of deep blue, soft fabric – so far so good.

I hold my breath and pull the garment out.

It's a dress, with long sleeves and a full coverage front, a tie at the waist and by the looks of it, the length will fall around my knees.

It's perfect.

"It's gorgeous," I breathe.

"You don't have to sound so shocked."

"I *am* shocked. I was seriously expecting at least a leg split or some awful attempt at getting my tits out or something."

She laughs long and loud, clutching her swollen belly as she does.

Pregnancy *becomes* Lucy, she's the most radiant and gorgeous pregnant woman I've ever seen.

"Don't worry, I'm not blind. I see your face every time I point out those types of outfits – I know they're not your thing."

"Then why do you keep suggesting them to me?" I cry in outrage.

"Because they'd look beautiful on you, Letty. Just because you don't see it, doesn't mean I can't."

I feel the blush heating my cheeks – I'm not good with any form of compliment, I never have been.

"And besides…" she winks at me, "you haven't seen the back yet."

I spin the dress around and grin. Now *this* type of plunging I can deal with.

The back drops down low and drapes at what I assume will be near the top of my bum.

I have no scars and nothing to hide back there and it's almost as though this dress was made just for me.

"It's amazing, thank you."

She waves her hand in front of her to indicate that it's no big deal at all, but I'm not having it. She's thought a lot about this outfit. I know she so desperately wants tonight to go well for me.

I don't date. Like, ever.

I'm not even entirely sure how I ended up agreeing to being set up on a blind date in the first place, my sly best friend and her equally as cunning husband must have caught me in a moment of weakness, but I'm here now, and looking far more respectable than I usually do – so I figure I may as well go and make the best of it.

"Seriously, Luce, it's beautiful. Thank you."

"You're welcome. Now put it on," she demands, glancing at her watch as she speaks, giving me a clear indication that I need to hurry up.

"Brown ankle boots," she hollers after me as I rush into my walk-in closet.

I emerge wearing the correct items of clothing and Lucy sighs in satisfaction.

"Perfect."

***

"Promise you'll be right next door?" I plead with Lucy and Emmett as we pull up outside the restaurant.

"I swear on my life," Lucy replies. "Now get out of the car and stop being such a chicken shit."

I've insisted they wait until either one of two things happen – one; I bail and need them to get me the hell out of there, or two; I hit it off with this guy and find my own way home.

I don't even feel bad about hijacking their evening for my own benefit – the two of them got me into this mess, it's the least they can do as far as I'm concerned.

"He's a good guy, Vi," Emmett reassures me in a manner far nicer than his hormonal wife.

"Okay, I can do this," I reply in a less than convincing tone.

"C'mon, woman, you've literally survived dying, and yet you're scared of a date?"

Lucy's right.

I *know* she's right, but that doesn't stop the heart that still feels foreign to me from beating erratically in my chest at the very thought of getting out of this car and walking inside.

"I can do this." I'm slightly steadier sounding this time so I open the door and step out while I'm still able to find the courage to go through with it.

Chapter Two

Rylan

I know that running late for a date isn't going to be the best first impression I've ever made, but I've got a pretty good excuse, and if the woman I'm meeting tonight doesn't understand that, then it was never going to work out anyway.

My job can be demanding, and I'm well aware that it's probably what's kept me from having any type of meaningful relationships with women thus far. That, and the lingering feeling something's missing whenever I'm in the presence of other people.

Ever since my sister passed away, I'm left constantly feeling like a piece of me is incomplete.

I've met nice women, but nothing ever feels as right as I know it should – so for years I never felt compelled to invite anybody new into my life.

I'm not expecting to walk into this restaurant tonight and find the solution to that problem, but a guy can dream.

I hear the tone indicating I have a text message as I throw myself into the driver's seat of my car. I stop at a red light and pull out my cell. I shake my head at the picture message I've just received from Emmett.

Emmett and I work together at the hospital, and with a bit of luck I'll be delivering his baby within the next two months.

He and his wife Lucy – they're the ones responsible for this set up tonight.

Emmett's sent me a picture of a woman I assume is Violet – my company for the evening. I can't see her face, and if I had to guess I'd say he took the picture of her as she walked towards the date I'm currently running late for.

The light turns green and I speed up a little; the thought of her sitting alone at a table is making me feel guilty.

After what feels like an eternity, I pull up outside and I must have some type of luck after all because there's a park right outside.

I take a deep breath before pushing the door open and jogging to the front of the restaurant.

Thanks to Emmett I know I'm looking for a woman with long dark hair, and a blue dress.

I'm glancing around as I give my name to the woman behind the desk and she points Violet out at the same moment that my eyes find her.

She doesn't look around as I approach from behind, and I still can't see her face.

I clear my throat in an attempt not to startle her, but still she jumps a fraction in her seat.

She turns slowly to face me and it's all I can do not to gasp as I see her face for the first time.

She's *so* beautiful, but not only that, she's oddly familiar.

I'm certain we've never met, but I feel drawn to her, like souls rekindling.

"Violet?" I question her, my voice sounding not at all like my own.

She looks at me as though she's seeing a ghost and her face pales visibly.

The doctor in me takes over.

"Are you okay?" I reach for her elbow on instinct; I'm worried that she's going to pass out, but for now at least she seems to be holding steady.

She's just staring at me in obvious shock.

She's caught up inside her own head right now, and I know that I won't reach her, no matter what I say. So I don't say anything, instead I crouch down next to her and wait.

It takes a full minute until she blinks once, twice, three times, before giving her head a little shake to clear it.

"Violet?" I repeat.

She reaches for her glass and takes a quick sip.

"I'm so sorry," she breathes as she sets it back down. "You gave me a fright. Rylan?" she questions me back, her eyes lingering on my face for a moment before trailing down my shoulder and arm to where my hand is still touching her.

I let her go hurriedly, as though I'm a teenager being caught doing the wrong thing.

"That's me," I tell her with a smile.

Her eyes are on my face again, as mine are on hers, and I watch in silent appreciation as her lips curve up to mirror mine.

An overwhelming sense of calm that I haven't felt in years settles over me, and I decide that now would be a good time for me to sit down.

Chapter Three

Violet

I would have known those eyes *anywhere* – I've dreamed about them nearly every night since I was twenty-one years old.

Three years ago, when I looked into them for the very first time in real life, it had shocked me beyond belief.

Much like right now.

He's saying my name and it's *just* like in my vision.

I can't breathe.

I don't know who this man is, but I know he means *something* to me.

He's literally the man of my dreams and that scares me half to death.

I know nothing about him, but he's here, saying my name and touching my arm and I still can't breathe.

"Are you okay?" he asks me, and I can hear the obvious concern in his voice.

'No, I'm not okay at all' I want to scream, but when I open my mouth, nothing comes out.

I can feel the anxiety clawing its way out of me and I know I only have seconds to get it under control.

I think of the technique one of my doctors taught me when I was younger.

Five, four, three, two, one...

I need to concentrate on five things I can see, four things I can touch, three things I can hear, two things I can smell and one thing I can taste.

Five... I can see *him,* the table, the waiter taking orders, cars on the street, my bag on the seat.

Four... I can touch *him,* the seat, the floor and the table-cloth.

Three... I can hear *him* saying my name, the people at the next table talking and the hum of energy from the kitchen.

Two... I can smell *him,* and garlic bread, and honestly, I'm not sure which smells better.

I can feel my breathing settling now as my body becomes more grounded and calm.

One... I can taste... my eyes immediately dart to his lips, but I grab my glass of orange juice before I do something stupid.

"I'm so sorry," I finally say as I put my glass back on the table. "You gave me a fright."

I look up and he's still watching me carefully.

"Rylan?" I ask, even though it's obviously him.

"That's me," he replies, his face lighting up with a smile so beautiful it actually pains me to look at it.

I find myself smiling back at him; like I don't even have a choice in the matter.

It's not lost on me that all five of my senses were drawn to *him* first and foremost, and considering I don't know him in the slightest, that's an unexpected revelation.

He sits opposite me and I'm overcome with a feeling that maybe my life is only just beginning right in this very moment.

***

"And that's why I was late," he replies with a shrug, only now getting around to explaining why he'd kept me waiting.

"You're an obstetrician?" I ask, surprise clearly colouring my voice.

We've been talking for over half an hour, and so far, I've managed to keep myself from asking him how or why it is that he frequents my dreams at night.

I've also managed not to freak out and panic again, but the more he talks the more I get a feeling of déjà vu that I can't explain.

He nods and smiles, acknowledging that it's somewhat of an unexpected field of medicine for him to be in.

He looks like a real man's man – not someone that looks at women's private parts all day, while periodically delivering little bundles of joy.

His shoulders are broad and strong, his golden skin is freckled from time spent in the sun and his hair is as dark as the night sky.

If I didn't already know he worked in the hospital, and someone had told me to guess, I would have gone with something like a builder or a farmer – something that required him to have strong, rugged hands.

He's tall and lean – he's very obviously physically fit, and I know I *really* need to stop looking at him.

"You got it, I'm an obstetrician," he confirms with a shrug.

"And you were delivering a baby..." I repeat his words back to him, still not quite believing.

He chuckles and the sound is warm and comforting.

I smile at him while I watch the curve of his mouth as the laughter falls from his lips.

"She came early. We weren't expecting her until next week, but really, at this point I should know better than to expect a baby to come on its due date."

"Did you know Emmett and Lucy are having a baby?"

He points to himself. "Who do you think is delivering it?"

I gape at him. "Seriously?"

He nods his head proudly.

"Wow... you *must* be good. You should have seen how long it took her to decide on a car seat. I can't even imagine the process she went through to pick a doctor... did she bring you in for a formal sit-down interview?"

He grins, and once again the breath is stolen from my lungs.

"I know you're joking, but you're actually not far off."

A realisation I'd previously missed appears front and centre in my mind.

"Hold the phone, so *she* knows you? That sneaky little she-devil gave me the distinct impression she *didn't* know you."

My eyes are narrowed now, and my finger is pointed at him in an incredibly accusing manner.

"Hey, don't shoot the messenger." He holds his hands up in surrender.

I make a pretend shooting motion with my finger, and he laughs – really laughs for the first time tonight.

It's a perfect sound and I'm already wishing I was funnier so I could say something that would let me hear it again.

"I can't believe she played me like that." I scowl half-heartedly.

He looks right into my eyes. His stare is strong and unwavering, and I almost shudder under the weight of it.

"Did she choose wrong?" he asks seriously.

I hold his gaze and shake my head, one small little movement that he doesn't miss.

She chose good – *really* good.

He's interesting, kind, funny, and somehow, manages to pull off this intense thing he has going, all the while looking like an absolute dream.

But the thing is, I'm not sure that Lucy and Emmett chose him at all.

I'm forced to think, that after nearly four years of dreaming of the deep blue eyes that are now focused on my face, watching me carefully, that perhaps this meeting was just meant to be.

I've never been a big believer in fate, because then I'd have to accept the fact that someone, somewhere deemed it my fate to suffer when others don't, but after spending tonight in his magnetising presence, I might have to rethink my views on the world.

"Well... good then," he replies, reminding me where I am and who I'm with, even though my eyes haven't left his for a moment.

The sight of him in my mind has become a sense of calm for me, a comfort even... and I hope to God that I'm reflecting my behaviour in a way that is appropriate for two strangers meeting, rather than someone greeting a familiar memory.

"Tell me something about you."

I refrain from groaning in response to his request.

I absolutely hate talking about myself. I despised the first day of school every year; the one where you had to stand up in class and tell the group a fun fact about yourself.

I would literally rather stick pins in my eyes than tell another 'fun fact'.

There's very little to tell about me that isn't going to get me *that* look. The look of sympathy.

I loathe the look of sympathy.

I don't want people to feel sorry for me, I want them to accept me for who I am and not what I've been through. I don't want to become my condition, but sometimes I fear I've done exactly that.

"What do you do for work?" he prompts when I don't reply.

I smile at the question because *that* is one I can answer – even if it's not with total honesty. Technically, I don't work – I volunteer, but he doesn't need to know that just yet.

"I work at an animal shelter."

His eyebrows raise in surprise. "That might be as rewarding as delivering babies."

"I actually helped deliver a whole litter just last week," I brag.

"Well then, here's to new life." He picks up his glass and holds it up to me.

I reach for my glass and clink it gently against his, repeating his sentiment back to him.

I spend the entire time it takes for our mains to arrive talking about the shelter and the quirky animals that come through, and he's either an excellent actor, or he's genuinely interested because he asks me questions the entire time.

I get to hear him laugh again and my insides feel all fuzzy and warm.

We eat in a comfortable silence and I'm aware that he's watching me as closely as I'm watching him.

I've already learned that he's the kind of person that eats each element on his plate separately, not starting the next type of food until the last one is finished. He's methodical even in his eating habits.

I, on the other hand, am quite the opposite, I eat a little piece of this, then that, then this again. It's the unrestrained artist coming out in me I think.

"I paint," I blurt the words out before I even consider the implication of them.

I only paint for me, and the reason I don't tell people about it is because the first thing they ask is if they can see my work.

He's watching me again – honestly, I'm not sure he ever stopped, and I can almost feel him rummaging around in my thoughts – like he somehow understands that even though I brought the topic up, I'm not entirely sure I actually want to talk about it.

"What do you paint?" he asks cautiously after a moment of silence.

I fiddle nervously with the gold ring that I wear on a chain around my neck.

"My feelings, my thoughts..." I shrug. "Whatever comes to me."

He nods for more than a few seconds, like he's processing the information.

"I bet they're incredible."

I wait for it – the 'I'd really like to see them sometime', but it doesn't come; he simply picks up his glass and takes another sip.

"That's a beautiful ring." He tilts his head in the direction of the ring I'm still playing with and I'm taken by surprise – he's as observant as he is intense.

I bring it up to my face so I can study it, as though maybe I've forgotten what it looks like all of a sudden.

"It was my aunt's. She gave it to me before she passed away."

And there I go again... speaking before I think, but much like before, he doesn't ask me questions that I don't want to answer.

"It matches your eyes beautifully," he simply replies.

I can feel myself blushing again. Even though he didn't technically give me a compliment, it still feels like one.

It does match my eyes – that's why she gave it to me. My Aunt Rita was more like a grandmother to me growing up, she was fifteen years older than my mother, and their parents – my grandparents, were both gone by the time I was born.

She was an absolute loon and I loved her dearly.

She lived long enough to see me get my new heart, and then she was gone, leaving behind a longing ache in my chest, the most wonderful memories, and a trail of wealth that gave my entire family more than we ever thought we'd have.

"You loved her." He's not asking a question, but merely reading my expression and stating a fact – it seems to be a skill of his.

We might not eat the same way, but we both appear to share the talent of reading people.

"I loved her very much. She was kind, kooky and very generous."

When she passed away, she left me the home I now live in along with a small fortune that will ensure I never want for a single thing. Auggie and Charlie have one each too.

She's the reason I can spend my time painting and volunteering without having to worry about how I'm going to pay the bills.

None of us had any idea that Rita was so well off, or that when she died, she'd leave everything to the five of us. She never had any children of her own, so my parents, my siblings and I, we were it for her.

"She gave me a house." The words come out without thought yet again.

I don't know what it is about him, but my walls keep slipping and I find myself telling him things I'd never normally consider telling a someone I just met.

Maybe it's because he doesn't feel like a stranger to me at all.

His eyes widen in surprise, and just when I expect him to question me further, he brings out the line I was expecting earlier, when I told him that I paint.

"I'd really like to see it sometime."

My heart is beating overtime at the very thought of having this beautiful man in my home, I'm scared, *so* scared to let people into my life.

This all feels like I've been thrown into a pressure cooker. The force is already building up, and I don't want it to explode, or the lid to lift and the air to escape. I just want to stay right here with him and let this pressure build.

I've never felt this comfortable and yet off kilter at the same time, but I think I like it – it feels like living.

"I think that might be okay," I tell him coyly.

He dips his head and grins, like that was exactly the answer he was hoping for, and for the first time in a long time, I think that maybe everything might be okay after all.

Chapter Four

Rylan

"This is a beautiful house."

It's an understatement – the huge Victorian home in front of me is as stunning as it is grand, but I've quickly come to learn that Violet isn't one for making a fuss, so I don't say anything more about it.

"I love it." She smiles as she glances up.

We're walking up the path to her front door, and there's nothing out here but us, the silence and the moonlight.

This whole evening has felt this way – like it's just been her and I, talking like neither of us had anywhere else in the world to be.

I glance at her again and shake my head in disbelief that *I'm* the guy that gets to bring her home tonight.

She *really* is a beautiful woman; I'd have to be blind not to see the obvious beauty in front of me, but it's not just about her pretty face, she radiates goodness and warmth too.

She's cautious – I can see that, but she's got a sense of freedom about her that I'm not sure even she knows what to do with.

We're strolling *so* slowly, dawdling even, and I get the impression that she doesn't want this night to end any more than I do.

I can't quite comprehend the feeling I have inside me when she's around. I feel... at peace. It's something I haven't experienced in a very long while, and I'm not ready to let it go just yet.

I glance down and brush the back of my hand against the back of hers. I feel like a teenager all over again, and it's a sentiment I welcome.

It feels like a stage of my life that I can manage right now – it's innocent and pure and there's no expectation on either of us to do anything more than just be here. I'm not walking her to her door with the hope that she'll invite me in and we'll have wild sex all night long.

It's not that I don't want to do that, because as much of a gentleman as I am, I'm exactly that, a *man* – but just not tonight.

Even if that was on her agenda, which I'm confident it's not, Violet deserves more than that, and so do I.

I take her hand in mine when we reach the steps – under the pretence that I'm helping her up them, and don't get me wrong, I *am* happy to help, but this contact is as much for my benefit as it is for hers. I've been dying to feel her skin against mine again ever since I touched her arm. The satisfied smile on her face makes me think that maybe she feels the same way I do.

Her hand is small and delicate in my much bigger one, and I like it. It feels *right*.

I don't let go when we reach her door, and neither does she.

We turn to face one another, and I'm struck again with just how pretty her eyes are.

They sparkle like cut crystal does in the sunlight. Even out here in the dark they shine, and when I look into them I get an inexplicable feeling that I'm not only looking at an important part of my future, but also somehow at my past.

It shocks me to my core that I feel this way about her after only a few short hours, but if there's one thing I've learnt from delivering babies into their parents' waiting arms, it's that a person's whole life can change in a mere fraction of a second.

"I'd really like to see you again."

Yet another understatement.

"Well... you've got my number." She shrugs.

She's nervous – she's not sure if I'm going to kiss her or not.

I step towards her and reach my free hand out slowly towards her face.

There's a strand of hair that seems to find its way across her forehead often, and I sweep it away and tuck it behind her ear.

I lower my lips to her forehead and place a soft kiss there.

She visibly shudders at the action and it makes me want to do it again.

I pull back, one of my hands resting on her jaw, the other still intertwined with her hand. She looks up at me. Her eyes are cautious but curious. She wants to be kissed.

She tilts her face up towards mine, and I slowly lower my lips to hers, pressing them together ever so gently.

Her free hand reaches for my neck and lightly tugs down, inviting me even closer. I go, willing and eager for more of her.

Her lips are so soft and smooth, and I can taste the mint she took from her handbag earlier.

I want more. God, do I want more, but instead I pull away, knowing that I haven't earnt more, not yet anyway.

"Thank you for dinner," she whispers into the small space between us.

"You're welcome." My reply comes out just as quietly.

I lean in and press my lips to hers once more, just quickly before I lose myself in her all over again.

"I'll call you," I promise as I take a step back.

I'm still holding her hand in mine, and as much as I don't want to let it go, I know it's time. I bring her fingers to my lips and kiss her skin one last time before I let go and reluctantly leave.

I watch her from my car. She unlocks her door and waves to me before going inside.

I look back up at the house as the lights come on and allow myself to acknowledge that my long lost feeling of contentment can be found inside those very walls.

***

I see Emmett coming from a mile away, and my feeble attempt to bury my face in my notes goes as expected – totally unsuccessfully.

"Dr. Wilder..." He says my name in the kind of way a voiceover might announce a character in a cheesy movie. "How was the date?"

He's raising his brows suggestively at me. I'm not sure why he doesn't just tell me how my date went, because I have a pretty strong hunch that Violet would have been straight on the phone to Lucy the moment I dropped her home.

I consider blowing him off, but I can't do it. The guy is just too likeable – he and Lucy both are, and right now his obvious excitement is infectious.

"It was good," I reply as a grin breaks out on my face, and I find that, surprisingly, I actually *want* to talk about my evening.

I don't know Emmett all that well, or him I, but he seems to know me well enough to realise that this revelation is a win, albeit a small one.

"She's pretty incredible once you get past her defences, huh?"

He may not know *me* all that well, but it seems he does know Violet, and cares a lot about her too. It's sweet, and I'm happy to know she has such good friends. There's something about her that makes me think she deserves them.

She's a guarded woman, but when her mask slips and you see the real her, it's a beautiful thing to witness.

She's a bit like me in a lot of ways; we're both what I would consider to be old souls. I don't know her story yet, but I get the feeling that she's lived through a lot more life in her twenty-five years than most people have.

"I had a really good time with her."

"You seeing her again?"

One thing I've learnt about Emmett is that he's as straight up and to the point as they come. He doesn't beat around the bush and I like that about him. I prefer to know where I stand with people.

I haven't had much in the way of friends in the past few years and there's something about the big man in front of me that makes me think that maybe I've found one.

"I hope so," I tell him, because honestly, I want nothing more than to see her again. The idea of peeling back another layer of Violet intrigues me in a way that nothing else does.

I'm looking forward to being back in her company already, and that's a *big* deal for me – I haven't looked forward to something that isn't work in a very long time.

"I plan to call her today."

"That's good..."

"I hope it will be."

He seems like he has more he wants to say, so I wait for him to get it off his chest.

"She's been through a lot, doc, so if you're going to see her again, don't expect it to be all smooth sailing." He's still wearing a smile, but I can tell this is a serious statement.

I nod as he walks away, his warning heeded.

This conversation has only enforced the feeling that there's something special about Violet – something that I know nothing about.

I stroll around aimlessly for a while after that; I'm not even rostered on, and I'm ninety percent confident I won't be having any unexpected deliveries today, but I still seem to find myself here anyway.

Wandering the halls has become therapeutic for me. It's bizarre really. Most people, after a trauma, will avoid places and things that remind them of that event, but apparently, I'm not wired right, because I don't operate that way.

I work in the same hospital that my sister passed away in. I still walk the same halls I walked as I tried to accept that she was really gone, and I still linger outside the window of the girl whom I never got to meet.

The girl with the crystal blue eyes...

A visual of Violet smiling and giggling softly last night, the deep dimples visible in her cheeks, hits me like a wrecking ball and I nearly drop to my knees.

She's looking down at the table, but when she glances up to meet my gaze, the same eyes from my memory are looking back at me.

***

It's funny how when you're doing something you shouldn't be, you feel like everyone is looking at you.

They aren't really, but the feeling of eyes on you is suddenly very real.

I know this is a total breach of her privacy, and that I could be fired for doing this, but there's just something about Violet that I need to know, and the more I think about her and her familiar eyes, the more concerned I become.

I've never been a person that's able to let things like this go – so here I am, risking my career, because there's something in a woman's eyes that makes me feel like I've found my way back home.

I type her name into the search bar and peer out my door once more before hitting 'enter'.

I'm pretty sure I mutter a curse word as her file appears on my computer screen.

It's a *mile* long; in fact, I'm not sure I've ever seen a medical history quite this large in all the years I've been practising. Violet Miller has had more hospital stays than I've had hot dinners and that can't mean anything good.

I don't want to violate her privacy any more than I've accepted I need to, but I can't help looking at the first entry ever made – the one from the day she was born.

My hands shake as I read the doctor's notes.

It's her heart.

I know without looking what the rest of this will say... open heart surgery, probably infections, more open heart surgery, medication... and eventually maybe a transplant.

She's twenty-five now, and I hope to God that she's already got the heart she needs. Considering her colouring and the spring in her step, I'm almost certain she has, and I breathe a deep sigh of relief because of it.

I find what I'm looking for in a matter of minutes – the reason I feel like I've seen her and those eyes of hers before is because I *have*.

The month and year leap out at me and slap me clean across the face.

She was here while my sister was dying.

She was here on the same date that brings me to the brink of insanity annually.

She was here when I began wandering the hallways not knowing where to turn.

She was here when I first watched the girl with the crystal blue eyes who looked like she was on the verge of death – she *was* that girl... she *is* that girl.

I don't even read the notes that accompany that particular hospital stay – it doesn't matter what they say, what matters is that it *was* her.

I close the file down as fast as I can and rest my head in my hands.

This only confirms what I already knew.

Violet is the girl with the beautiful eyes. The girl who gave me hope in the darkest of all my hours, and I don't know if I'm more shocked with the revelation, or the fact that I didn't put it together sooner.

Chapter Five

Violet

"Has he called you yet?"

I roll my eyes at my best friend's ridiculous persistence.

"It's not even midday; give the guy a chance, would you?"

"He had a great time. It sounds like you two really hit it off."

I groan. "How on earth do you know he had a good time?"

"Emmett saw him at work, so he quizzed him, then he called me. Duh."

Of course he did. I don't know why I would have expected anything less – frankly I should probably just be grateful that Lucy didn't go ahead and call him herself.

"You two have been watching too many of those love match shows. You're both totally out of control, you know that, right?"

She laughs, and the sound is soft and tinkling.

She doesn't say anything more and we both know it's only a matter of time before I crack.

"Fine." I let out a resigned sigh. "Are you going to tell me what he said or not?"

Lucy doesn't require any further encouragement before she eagerly launches into a total re-enactment of the encounter.

I know her and Emmett well enough to know that the details of this story will be strongly inflated and possibly entirely inaccurate, but still, I listen with bated breath and all the excitement of a teenager talking about her first boyfriend. Because frankly, he might not be my boyfriend just yet, but he *is* near the top of a very short list of dates that I've had in my twenty-five years.

"Did you tell him about... you know, your heart and stuff?" Lucy asks me quietly and I feel a pang of guilt in my gut.

It's not that I think I owe him the story – not yet anyway, if I see more of him, then yeah... I'll need to explain to him the reality of my life.

But not having told him yet *isn't* why I feel guilty.

I feel guilty because of the reason I didn't tell him.

I didn't tell him because he's the man from my dream... my premonition, my life flashing before my eyes... whatever you want to call it... *he's* the one.

He's the one whose eyes stayed with me as I found my way back to life instead of disappearing into death.

He's the one who I've dreamed of nearly every night since.

I don't know what I would have said. I have no idea what I could possibly say to him that wouldn't send him running for the hills – so instead I said nothing.

There's also guilt because I've never told Lucy all of this.

She's my best friend, has been since we were babies, and this is the one and only thing I've never shared with her.

I don't even know why. Maybe one day I will bring her in on my secret, but for now at least, I know I'm not ready.

The only person I've talked about those moments with is Auggie, and suddenly I'm filled with an overwhelming desire to talk to my big sister.

"I didn't tell him," I respond quietly. "I will... if it goes anywhere, I'll tell him."

"I know you will, Letty."

"I still can't believe you forgot to mention that you actually know him," I grumble, hoping that I'll succeed in changing the subject.

"Well, technically, he knows my lady bits better than he knows me, so I didn't think I needed to mention it."

I groan again. "I really did not need a visual of the man I was kissing last night, looking at your lady bits."

"Um... back the truck up. *Kissing*? Now who's holding out on information, huh? You conveniently forgot to mention that you were locking lips with the hot doctor now, did you?"

I intentionally left that part out when I was texting Lucy last night. She'd barely managed to refrain from asking me five thousand questions when I let her and Emmett know they were relieved of their chaperone duties, and the minute I got home she jumped right back into it.

Lucy is *all* about the questions.

I laugh into the phone. "Cut the fake outrage, I'm telling you now."

"Oh, you bet your ass you are. I want all the details, right now."

I smile and revel in the feeling of being normal, even just for a few moments.

***

"Hey, stranger." I lean in and whisper hoarsely in August's ear as I approach from behind her.

She startles so easily, and I just can't help myself.

"I told you to stop doing that to me!" she cries once she realises it's me and not some creep trying to hit on her.

"And I keep telling you that I've lived this long for a reason, and if driving my sister crazy isn't one of them, then I just don't know what it is I'm meant to do with my life."

"You *really* need a boyfriend," she tells me as I sit down opposite her.

I smirk. "Well if I *did* have a boyfriend it would have made my date last night pretty awkward now, wouldn't it?"

Her jaw drops. "Did I just hear the word *date* come out of your mouth?"

"You did."

"Oh my God, who? Where? How did this happen? Who is he? When can I meet him?"

I take a sip of her coffee. "Calm down."

"But I have *so* many questions."

I laugh. She wouldn't be August if she didn't. Between my best friend and my sister, I could spend the rest of my life answering questions.

"It was a blind date, courtesy of Lucy and Emmett."

"How the hell did they get you to agree to that? I've been trying for years." She pouts at me.

"Does it really matter?"

"I tried to get you to go out with that guy I met in class and you wouldn't do it."

I roll my eyes. "Focus, Auggie."

She's not really listening to me, she's picking the information she wants out of my words, while ignoring everything she deems irrelevant.

"Who was the guy?"

She scowls at me when she reaches for her coffee and it's not there.

I hand the cup back and grab one of the little packets of sugar from the jar in the centre of the table.

I'm nervous, and when I'm nervous I fiddle with things... anything to keep my hands busy.

"That's actually what I wanted to talk to you about..."

She must notice that I'm uneasy about it because she puts down her cup and gives me her full attention.

"What did he do?" she demands.

August may be a lot of things, but deep down I know she'd go to the ends of the earth to hunt someone down if they hurt me. Thankfully her services won't be required today.

"It's nothing like that."

"Why don't you tell me how it is then?" She narrows her eyes at me.

I go back to picking at the label on the sugar packet. "Do you remember back before my transplant when my heart stopped?"

"I think I'm familiar," she answers, her lips tight.

No one in my family likes talking about that time in my life.

It took me a long time to comprehend just how close they'd come to losing me.

Hearing that my whole family had sat in a waiting room for hours with no clue if I was alive or dead was absolutely heart breaking.

"Do you remember me telling you about what happened... what I saw?"

We haven't talked about this for four years, so I'm half expecting her to have no recollection of it at all; she is Auggie after all.

"You seriously think I'd forget my little sister's vision of her future?"

I shrug.

"I remember, Vi. The baby, the guy with the blue eyes..."

"You called him the man of my dreams," I prompt her.

She looks proud of herself. "I did."

"I never told you this, but I saw him... in person, he was outside in the hallway when I woke up from my transplant."

Her eyes widen, and I can tell she's about to bombard me with questions.

"I didn't tell you because I knew you'd freak out, and to be honest, I wasn't entirely sure I didn't dream the whole thing up," I explain before she has the chance to speak.

"Why are you telling me this now?"

I don't answer her right away.

She reaches across the table and pulls the now shredded packet from my hands.

"Spill it, Vi."

"It was *him*...my date was with him," I whisper.

I hear her gasp.

"You've got to be shitting me?" She gapes at me in disbelief.

I huff out a little laugh and shake my head. "I shit you not."

"How? What? I don't get it…. what? But how? I can't deal, I just can't…"

She's rambling now, and I almost suggest my five, four, three, two, one method to her, but think better of it.

Auggie needs information and she needs it right now.

"He's a doctor. He works at Royal West with Emmett; so that could explain why he was there in the hallway after my transplant," I offer.

"Hold the phone. He's a *doctor*?" she asks quickly, and I laugh. Just like that, August's back.

"*Yes*, he's a doctor, and yes he's handsome, tall *and* he's a gentleman, before you ask."

"Holy crap, did you marry him?"

I know she's joking, but just those words put me right back in the pressure cooker.

I can't explain why, but all I know is that this is so important, *all* of it – I can feel it in my bones.

"You're sure it's him?"

"I've got no doubt. I'd know those eyes anywhere."

"Well… heck…"

It's not often in my life that I've seen August lost for words, but right now is one of those moments.

"Maybe he was one of your doctors; you said it yourself that he works there… you could have woken up for a while and seen him before they got you back under. That can happen, right?"

It's not a bad theory, and it's one I have considered over the past few years, but I've always known it's not what happened.

"He's an obstetrician, so that'd be a little weird."

She nods in agreement.

"Okay, so did you tell him?"

She says it as though it'd be as casual as mentioning the weather.

"Of course I didn't tell him! He'd probably submit me for a psych evaluation."

"He might be a spiritual guy..." She shrugs.

He'd have to be a little more than spiritual to think this was normal.

"I haven't told him anything about *anything* yet. It was just one date, Auggie."

"Has he called you today?"

I groan. "You sound just like Lucy. *No*. He hasn't called yet. Maybe he never will. I probably wouldn't. I've got more baggage than a freaking airplane's cargo hold."

She raises her brows at me. "You done with your pity party?"

"I'm not sure." I pout back at her.

For someone who basically lives in a constant state of self-involvement, August has always been the first to tell me to snap out of it when I'm feeling down on myself.

Whether that's because she doesn't like me feeling that way, or because she'd rather I was focusing on her instead of me, I'm not sure, but either way, it's hard to feel too down in the dumps when she's around.

"Don't be such a sad sack. Besides, think of it this way, if he doesn't call you, you can't even blame it on your heart, because you didn't tell him about it."

"Thanks for that. So if he doesn't call it's just due to the fact that I'm terrible company then?"

She winks at me. "*Exactly*."

"That makes me feel *so* much better," I deadpan.

She smirks at me. "Don't say I never do anything for you."

We sit in silence for a moment as the drink I ordered is brought over to our table.

"So, what are you going to do, Vi?"

I don't have an answer for that. I can't possibly. I don't even know if Rylan wants to see me again, and until I do, it's all a moot point.

It sure seemed like he was interested, but considering I don't know a single thing about romance with boys, let alone men, I really can't be sure.

I don't particularly want to agonise over a decision that may never be required from me at all.

"I think I'm just going to wait and see what happens."

She nods in acceptance and sips from her cup again.

"I still can't believe it's him." She breathes out a breath of disbelief, and I know exactly how she feels.

I'd felt the same way when I looked into his eyes last night.

"I know you don't really believe in fate and things that are 'meant to be', but it might be time you started to think again." She says the words quietly, and that's how I know she means them.

And to be honest, she's not wrong about it either.

One short evening with Rylan Wilder has made me re-think everything I thought I was sure about.

Chapter Six

Rylan

I don't know how I'm supposed to feel after what I've just seen.

I know damn well that most men would run a mile when faced with a woman that lives with the things Violet does every single day.

But then I've never really been like 'most men'.

I'm shaken by what I saw, undoubtedly, but what's really rattled me most is the fact that Violet is *the girl*. She's the one I watched all those years ago, and I don't know how to process that, or what to make of it.

Strange coincidences happen in the world, and I get that, but this doesn't feel like one of those times.

I've experienced instances in my life where everything has just felt like it's falling into place – like I'm exactly where I'm supposed to be.

I felt that way when I stood outside her room all those years ago, after my sister died.

It scared me then, and the thought of it still confuses me now.

I felt it again last night, when I held Violet's hand and kissed her under the moonlight. Only this time, I didn't feel fear – I felt relief.

I've got so much to learn about her, and her, I, but hell, I want to know it *all*.

She's probably been put in the too hard basket by people her entire life, and I don't want to be the guy that does that to her too.

Hell, I'm not even sure if it actually bothers me.

I'd be lying if I said I hadn't thought about her situation at all. I don't have any real idea what her condition is like, or how her heart is responding to whatever treatment she's received over the years.

There's no quick fix. There are procedures, surgeries and medication – but the battle she's facing is a lifelong one. Even a new heart can't last her forever, if she's got one, that is.

I desperately want to open her file again and find out her entire medical history, but I can't.

I like Violet. I respect her, and I've already violated her privacy far more than I ever should have.

I vow to myself that I'll never go behind her back for anything like this ever again. If she wants me to know something – she'll tell me herself.

I know it's the right decision, but it's one that doesn't help ease my apprehension in the slightest.

I'm scared for her. I don't know how I couldn't be.

I felt something for that woman last night, something *real,* and if I can feel like that after only a few short hours, I can't even imagine what a whole day with her could do to my head.

I want to find out everything there is to know. I want to spend many more days talking and laughing, but the harsh reality is, I don't know how many days she's got. I doubt anyone does.

The doctor in me tries to analyse the situation with rational thought and logic, but already I'm past the point of rational when it comes to Violet.

I know there's no real choice for me.

I *have* to see her again.

She evoked emotion in me that I'd long thought was dead and buried, and I need to feel that way again.

I *need* to see her and her beautiful eyes… and above all else I need to figure out exactly why she already feels so vitally intertwined with my life.

Chapter Seven

Violet

"Hello?"

My voice comes out breathless and rushed as I answer my phone.

I know it's him on the other end of the line, and that knowledge makes my heart beat frantically against my rib cage, like it's trying to make its escape.

"Hey, Violet, it's Rylan..."

"You called," I reply stupidly, because frankly, I'd convinced myself that he wasn't going to.

"Did you really think I wouldn't?"

I shrug before realising he can't actually see the action.

I really am terrible at this dating thing.

"I wasn't sure, but I hoped you would..." More truths – they seem to just fall from my lips where he's concerned.

"I like that." I can hear the smile in his voice.

I'm lying on my back across my bed, my legs dangling off the side, and I feel the way I imagine the teenage girl in movies does when she's talking to the captain of the football team.

My heart is racing and there's butterflies going crazy in my stomach.

"Well I like that you called," I reply lamely.

He laughs lightly down the phone.

Neither of us seems to know what to say, and this is beyond awkward, but there's still nowhere I'd rather be than here, with him on the other end of the phone.

"I had a really good time last night."

"I heard." I giggle.

Lucy and Emmett are an unstoppable force of nature. There was never any way that Rylan was going to be able to escape unscathed.

He laughs again, louder this time and it makes my smile grow wider. "Emmett isn't really one for personal boundaries, is he?"

"Pffft." I snigger. "You think *he's* bad, you should hear what I've been dealing with since I walked in the door last night. Lucy's been asking every five minutes if you've called me yet."

"You'll have to tell her I'm sorry for keeping her waiting, I ended up at work all day."

"I'll be sure to pass that on." I laugh. "So did you have any deliveries today?"

"Not today... actually I didn't really *need* to be at work, but you'll probably learn that taking time away from the hospital isn't something I'm very good at."

I bite down on my lip, my smile so wide I'm a little afraid my face might split in half.

He's just implied that I will get to know him better, and whether or not he intended for it to come across that way or not, it's how I've taken it.

"You think I'll get to learn about you?"

"I hope so, Violet. I plan on learning a lot about you." His voice sounds hoarse, and there's a sincerity there that I can't possibly deny.

I can understand in this moment why people are so eager to date and to fall in love. This feeling of excitement and euphoria is like nothing I've ever experienced.

For the first time in a long time, I welcome it; I think that maybe I might finally feel ready to put myself out there.

Rylan is like no one I've ever met before, and he's a far cry from the guys I've been turned down by in the past.

He's mature, kind and gentle. He's not some silly little boy, he's a man.

"What are you doing right now?"

I glance at the clock next to my bed. It's seven on Saturday evening, and my plans consist of nothing at all, as do most of my Saturday nights.

"I'm lying on my bed, with not a thing on the agenda."

There's silence for a moment, and when he speaks I can hear the smile in his voice.

"Do you want to go for a walk with me?"

I don't even have to think about it, I've never heard a better idea in my life.

***

"This is my favourite spot. I've seen a lot of places, but nothing comes close to this."

He's right, this *is* a beautiful sight.

We're up on a clifftop along the coast, and considering it was only a half-hour walk up here, I don't know how I've never done it before.

I'm a little short of breath, and while it's frustrating, it's nothing out of the ordinary for me.

The sun is beginning to lower in the sky; soon it'll set. The ocean is calm and glistening, and the clean waves are crashing against the sandy shore.

The smell of the sea air is so relaxing; I close my eyes for a moment and just breathe it in.

That's one positive about coming so close to death – you learn to appreciate the little things.

I'm not sure I would have ever stopped to smell the flowers, or lie in the long grass, or chat with strangers if not for the condition I've lived with for twenty-five years.

I don't take a single moment for granted anymore, and I certainly wouldn't dream of taking this particular tick of the clock for anything other than the miracle it is.

I breathe deeply and take a second to acknowledge just how lucky I am to be here, alive and well, and when I open my eyes, Rylan's looking at me with a stare that asks so many questions, but at the same time, understands so much.

"It's sort of sobering up here, isn't it?"

I nod my head and look out at the horizon. "I've never felt so small or insignificant."

Out here in the cool evening air, with no one else around, is so refreshing. It makes me realise what a little part of the universe I really am.

In my world, everything is always about me and my health, my good days and my bad ones; it's all about my heart.

But not out here... out here I'm just a woman looking at the sea.

Most people wouldn't like the idea of being a no one, but for the most part I'd be happy to be of little significance.

All my life I've felt like some type of experiment. No one ever knew what to expect from one day to the next and it was always a case of trying something out and then waiting to see what happened.

It's been one big high-risk game of trial and error, where the ideal outcome is that I live, and in the worst case – I die.

"There's some serious thinking going on in that head of yours."

He startles me; for a moment I forgot he was right here next to me.

I can feel the weight of his stare on me again and I can't help but marvel at the fact that when faced with such an incredible view, he's still choosing to look at me instead.

"I've got a lot to think about," I say as I turn to face him.

"Anything I can help you with?"

His smile is so sweet and genuine I seriously consider taking him up on his offer.

I *could* tell him. I could open my mouth and let the words all fall out. It's not that I don't trust him with the information, but I can't bring myself to taint this picture-perfect moment.

The golden sun is sinking out of view behind him and I don't want to ruin this small lapse in time.

"I think one day you might be able to."

He smiles at me and looks down at his shoes before meeting my eyes again.

I'm learning this is how he reacts when I give him an answer that he likes – one that really speaks to his soul.

"Violet?" he says quietly as he looks out at the ocean.

"Yeah?"

"You could *never* be insignificant."

He reaches for me and as the sun disappears from sight, I'm left standing in the dim light with my hand held in his.

Chapter Eight

Rylan

I can't even remember the last time I had what I would call a *good* dream.

It's not that my nights are filled with nightmares or the stuff from horror films, but I haven't had that feeling where you wake up smiling in a really long time.

But I'm smiling now, and I know Violet is the reason for that.

Last night was even better than the first we spent together.

I can't recall a time where I've felt so content in someone's presence.

She's not like others. She's got more depth than half the people I've met thus far in life put together, and when I talk, she listens, *really* listens to the words I'm saying... but more than that, I think she understands my reasons for saying them too.

She's funny, considerate and so, *so* beautiful.

I can't stop myself from looking at her. I know she notices it; the stain of blush on her cheeks assures me she's aware, but she's not once complained.

I smile again as I picture her hand in mine. My skin still tingles in the spot where it met hers. It's unbelievable really; I never thought a walk and a scoop of ice cream could bring me so much happiness.

Happiness... it's something I wasn't sure I'd truly experience again. My sister dying sort of sucked all the joy from my life, but ever since I met Violet, I feel it again.

It's there.

And when I kissed her goodbye, under the stars and the moon once again, I'd felt the last of my reservations slip away.

She is the girl with the blue eyes – the girl who gave me hope.

I've got no choice but to see where this goes, and even if I did have the ability to choose, I know that she's what I'd decide on.

This is one of those situations in life where it seems as though it's less about me making a choice, than it is about a choice making me.

I've had moments since I made this realisation where I don't understand why I couldn't have met her *then*, why we couldn't have had the past three years to get to know each other instead of just the past few days.

The past three days have been better than I thought was possible, whereas I've *endured* these past three years.

There's no other way to describe it. I get by okay now, but when I'm with Violet, it doesn't feel like just 'getting by', it feels like living.

I realise in an instant that it doesn't matter why or how this has all come to be, all that matters is that she's here – that she's in my life *now*.

Maybe it is fate – Daisy was always a big believer in fate. Maybe this is our time.

Maybe I wasn't meant to meet her three years ago... neither of us were in a place where we could have been ready for another person in our lives... but I think we're both there now.

I think I'm ready for not only someone, but for *her*... I hope to God that she's ready for me too.

She's on my mind so constantly, there's no space for darkness anymore.

Once again, *she* is my light.

Chapter Nine

Violet

I scrawl the word 'happiness' on the back of the canvas and collapse into my chair with a thud.

I'm so totally exhausted, but at the same time, I've never felt so alive.

My eyes can barely stay open, and I know I'll be paying for pulling this all-nighter for days to come, but as I turn the canvas around and look at it one more time, I know it was all worth it.

It's everything he's making me feel, exposed and raw on the surface in front of me.

I've felt a lot of things in my life, but never anything that's come close to this.

I can't tell if this is what it always feels like when you meet someone you like, or if this is something more than that... I'm too inexperienced to know.

My gut tells me it's more – that this is *so* much more than some crush, but I'm scared to say it out loud, I'm scared to do anything that might jinx it. The last thing I want is to tar this with my usual bad luck brush.

I want this to be real.

I remember the way Lucy was when she met Emmett, I'd never seen her so smitten. She fell in love with that man the moment she met him, and she still loves him just as fiercely now.

I've never given much thought to the concept of soul mates before, but when I look at the two of them, it's a hard notion to deny.

I've wondered for a long time if I'd ever find love. I know it's worried my mum a lot too.

I guess as a parent, you sort of just assume that one day your children will find someone to cherish them. Most parents probably just hope that when their future son or daughter-in-law is chosen, that they're a good person.

My mum's worries run a little deeper... as do mine.

There are all the normal considerations, like personality, looks and chemistry, but I've got the added pressure of finding someone who is equally as considerate as they are good look-ing, and as accepting as they are funny.

Not everyone out there has it in them to love those of us who aren't quite 'normal', and finding someone who loves me, despite the state of my heart, was never going to be a simple task.

I think of myself as a bit of a hazard.

Loving me carries so much risk. I read a book when I was younger, and the main girl talks about herself and her illness as being like a grenade – that one day she'll blow up and that everyone in her life will be casualties.

I feel that on a deep level. That's the reality of my life a lot of the time. I can't fathom that the value of knowing me is worth the risk of the fallout from losing me.

Mum, Dad, Charlie and Auggie, they don't really have an option... you can't choose your family, and they're stuck with me whether they like it or not.

Lucy though... she's here by choice. Nobody tells Lucy what to do – and believe me, I've tried. She's as stubborn as an old goat and there's no way she's going anywhere.

She really is the best friend a girl could ask for.

And then there's Rylan... I know we've only been on two dates, but it feels like so much more than that.

We share a connection.

I know I'm going to have to tell him soon... and when I do, he'll probably flee. Any sane person probably would.

I hope for his sake that he does.

I can already tell he's an incredible man. He's got so much going for him, and his future shines so bright it's like looking directly into the sun.

He deserves someone who can give him so much more than I can.

A family, good health, time...

None of those things are promised to me.

Not one doctor has been able to tell me what *my* future holds.

There's statistics and averages, possibilities and chances, but none of those things are guaranteed and they're certainly not certain.

All I can do is hope for the best.

I guess I'm one of the lucky ones when I think about it.

I lasted twenty-one years before my heart really tried to kick the bucket, and it took less than a year to find a new heart for me – which, in the scheme of things, isn't all that long.

I've made it three years past transplant now, and the chances of my body rejecting the organ are significantly reduced.

There's a long list of risks and problems that can arise from having a heart transplant, but so far, I've got by okay – a couple of infections my body had trouble fighting off, a little bit of emotional trauma, and one significant hospital stay... but all in all, it's been pretty uneventful in comparison to the year that preceded my transplant.

I don't know how long this heart will last me, or whether it might just give up on me one day... I don't know if I'll need another transplant or if medical science will evolve to the point where there's another option.

It's all the unknown. My whole life is one big unknown.

Rylan has everything going for him. He's smart, attractive, kind and funny – he's a doctor for crying out loud.

He could have any woman he wanted.

I know that worrying about this is probably totally unnecessary, but I can't seem to help it – maybe I did inherit some personality traits from my mother after all.

I know that Rylan might decide to wake up tomorrow and never contact me again. Rationally, I understand that, but I've got my hopes up and for someone who has spent her whole life *not* getting her hopes up, this is a big deal for me.

It's clear there's only one thing for it.

I have to tell him.

I need to make sure he's fully informed about me and my life before I let myself or him get anymore invested.

Sometimes the only way to move forward is by going back.

***

"I'm going to tell him."

Lucy looks up from her lunch in surprise. "What? Already?"

I stare at her in confusion. I could have sworn this was the same Lucy that was telling me I shouldn't keep it a secret any longer.

"I thought you wanted me to tell him?"

"I *do*," she blurts out quickly. "I *totally* think you should tell him. I'm just surprised that you're agreeing to it so early in the piece... that's all."

"I mean... I dunno... I think he needs to know." I shrug.

She narrows her eyes at me as she sets her knife down, and now I know I'm in for it. Lucy – especially a pregnant Lucy, doesn't let *anything* come between her and her food. I watched Emmett attempt to take a French fry off her plate the other day and he was lucky to make it out of there without her fork stabbed into his arm.

"What do you mean by that?"

I avoid her stare and push my own food around my plate.

"*Violet*..." she warns me when I don't answer.

"I just think he should know what he's getting himself into, okay? I'm damaged goods, and I'd hate for him to start to like me and then change his mind once he found out. I'd rather it happen before then."

I'm looking right at her now so I don't miss the softening of her eyes.

"Oh, Letty... that's not going to happen..."

"You don't know that."

She goes to repeat her statement of denial again but stops herself. "You know what, you're right. I *don't* know, but I do know that he's a good man, a really good man... *and* a doctor – a little bit of a heart defect shouldn't be able to scare him off."

I can't help but laugh at Lucy's downplaying of my condition. I know she's not being serious and I also know she's achieved exactly what she set out to do – she's made me smile.

"Please don't write him off just yet, let *him* be the one who decides to stay or go – don't make that choice for him."

She's right. I'm doing what has become habit for me – I'm expecting the worst.

Maybe just this once I should try hoping for the best instead and see what comes of it.

I'm staring at my plate, quietly contemplating what to do when she speaks again.

"You really like him then?"

Once again, she's hit the nail on the head.

Telling him is as much about me as it is about him.

Yes, I want him to know the whole truth, so he can make his own choices, but I also want him to know so that I can limit the damage to my own heart if he walks away. I'm aware that I'm getting invested in him already, and I don't want to catch any more feelings if he's just going to leave me.

"I've never felt this way, Luce. I'm really scared."

She reaches for my hand and gives it a squeeze. "It's good to be scared sometimes... it means you're alive."

I like that she doesn't try to dig for more information, I know that she will, but for now she knows I need the support of my best friend, not the full Spanish Inquisition.

"I've got a good feeling about him, Violet."

I've got lots of feelings about him too – but that doesn't help my nerves in the slightest, in fact if anything, I think it makes it worse.

Chapter Ten

Rylan

To: Rylan
From: Violet
Okay, there's something I have to ask...

I'm smiling at my phone like some kind of crazy person. Thankfully I'm in the privacy of my exam room, so no one can see me anyway, but honestly, I'm not sure anything could wipe the smile off my face right now – not even my colleagues thinking I'd lost my mind entirely.

This light-hearted banter has been going on for the past hour or so, and it's lucky really that I'm here in my spare time again and not on shift, because I'm not sure I'd be able to focus on anything other than Violet and her messages.

My phone beeps indicating another text has arrived, and I smile even bigger as I anticipate her question.

To: Rylan
From: Violet

So you look at... you know... *lady parts* all day... I mean wouldn't you get sick of seeing that... like in your personal life?

I laugh out loud at that one.

I can almost see her blushing from here. She's adorable really.

To: Violet

From: Rylan

You know what; it *is* just vagina all day around here... it's really a wonder I haven't turned gay over it.

I wait for her reply almost anxiously. I'm not sure how she'll respond to my teasing.

To: Rylan

From: Violet

You just made me spit a mouthful of water across the room, so touché... I'll give you ten points for that one. I'll also take that as a no to my question.

I'm thinking about how incredible she is when another text comes through before I have a chance to reply.

To: Rylan

From: Violet

P.s. While I have no issue with gay men, I'm really glad you aren't one.

She's funny too.

No one has made me smile like this in years, and here she is, making me laugh without even trying.

I'm dying to see her again; she's like an addiction I can't satisfy.

To: Violet

From: Rylan

I like you, Violet Miller.

Her reply is instantaneous.

To: Rylan

From: Violet

I like you too, Rylan Wilder.

***

"What are you doing tomorrow?"

Her eyes are bright and excited and it's infectious. When she smiles, I smile.

I've got a strong suspicion that whatever Violet was feeling, I'd feel it too. It's like there's a direct link between her emotions and mine.

It might be invisible to the eye, but I *feel* it... it's there, and while it terrifies me, it also excites me like nothing else.

"I've got the day off tomorrow actually."

I don't know why she's asking, but it doesn't matter, if there's anything on offer, I'll take it.

I had to work the last two days, and they were the longest days of my life. Knowing I had a date with Violet waiting for me tonight made the hours seem to drag on forever. I can't recall a time when I was actually more eager for something outside of the hospital, rather than something within it.

"Perfect." She grins at me as I open the door into the bowling alley – our destination for the evening. "I've got somewhere I want to take you."

She's so pretty when she smiles. It lights up her whole face and causes those deep dimples in her cheeks that I'm beginning to crave.

"I'm intrigued."

"I'll pick you up, okay?"

"Tour guide *and* chauffer, huh?"

"At your service." She winks.

She strolls off ahead of me and I find myself following along behind her like a little puppy dog.

"Are you not going to tell me where we're going?"

She turns back to face me, her eyes sparkling with mischief.

"I bet you're one of those people that hate surprises, am I right?"

She's *exactly* right. I thoroughly dislike them, but I'm not about to tell her that.

I like to have a plan. I get enough of the unknown and unexpected with my job, so I tend to avoid it in my personal life – when I actually bother to have a personal life that is, but I already know I'll make some type of exception for her.

"Me?" I make a show of balking at her statement. "I *love* surprises."

She giggles, and I'm filled with warmth. "You're a terrible liar."

She's right about that too. I always have been... my sister always said I couldn't lie to save my life.

It bothered me as a child, but now I like to think of it as one of my better qualities.

I give the young girl behind the counter the name on the bowling lane I've pre-paid for. Violet has been making a good show of insisting that she was going to be treating *me* to this date but there was no way I was going to let her hand over a cent.

It's not that I'm stuck in the dark ages, but in my mind, when a man is courting a woman, *he* should pay for the privilege.

That's how my grandfather courted my grandmother and how my father courted my mother.

It's the way I want to do it too.

Violet pouts at me when she realises what I've done. "Rylan! I told you *I* was paying today."

"You're going to have to be faster than that then." I wink at her and she scrunches up her nose in frustration.

She hurriedly hands her credit card to the girl. "I'm paying for the snacks then."

The girl, 'Kate' according to her name badge, grimaces. "Ummm... he's kind of already ordered *and* paid for all of that too..."

I watch Violet's jaw drop as she turns back to me. "You're impossible... we had a deal."

I shrug and grin. "You might have *thought* we had a deal... I never agreed to let you pay, Violet. Call me old fashioned, but I want to take you out – so I pay, okay?"

"Girl, you should just let him... I mean hell, I wouldn't say no if some cute guy wanted to spoil me."

I shoot Violet a 'see' look.

Violet blushes as she looks between me and Kate, who is now setting our bowling shoes down on the counter.

"Well I can see I'm outnumbered." She sighs. "Fine, thank you, it's very sweet – albeit totally unnecessary," she adds in a grumble.

There's a small smile playing on the corner of her lips and I know she can't hold this grudge for long.

"C'mon..." I grab both pairs of shoes before slinging my arm around her. "I've got a real deal for you."

"And what would that be?"

We approach our lane and I look at her, unable to keep the huge smile off my face. "If I win, you have to tell me where we're going tomorrow."

She laughs. "And if *I* win?"

I think about it for a moment. "If you win... I'll let you pay for our next date."

She blushes again, and her lips turn up in a coy smile – I know she's thinking about the fact that I've just committed to another date, and while she seems pretty damn happy about it, this deal is still very clearly stacked in my favour.

She holds out her hand for me to shake. "Alright then, deal."

***

"You could have told me you were a pro," I grumble. "I got hustled."

She giggles gleefully – I think she's still pretty pleased with herself about her win.

Actually, *win* doesn't quite cut it, she whipped my butt good and proper.

"A deal's a deal, Dr. Wilder. I get to pay for the next date."

It's me who's pouting now.

That'll teach me for underestimating her – I'd been so sure I was going to win the game *and* our little bet.

She's walking backwards so that she's facing me, as we stroll through the park.

I want so badly to find out about her heart; she's so radiant and filled with life, I almost wonder if I looked at the wrong patient's file. If it weren't for the fact that I've seen her, frail and extremely unwell with my very own eyes, I'd probably have decided by now that I *had* made a mistake.

I won't ask her though. I can't. Not without revealing I violated hospital policy or that I somehow know her from a hospital corridor years ago.

Neither of those things are something I want to share at the moment, or perhaps ever, so I just have to wait... wait and hope that she'll trust me enough to tell me when she's ready. There's so much more to her than just her heart, and I can't blame her for wanting to share who she really is as a person before she's forced to confess the thing that's probably defined her for her whole life.

Maybe it's better this way – that I'll learn about her first and her heart later.

I want to know everything about her – the *real* her... and this is probably the best chance I'm going to get.

"Hey... do you want to come and have dinner with me?" she asks unexpectedly, breaking me from my thoughts.

"You mean at your house?"

I'm yet to set foot inside Violet's house, but I want to so badly I have to stop myself from yelling the word 'yes' at her.

"Yeah... I've got a heap of food; it's kinda hard to cook the right amount for just me... I mean if you're not busy..."

She's rambling, and as soon as I recognise it's because she's nervous I'll say no, I almost *do* yell the word at her.

"That sounds perfect, Violet," I interrupt her chatter.

"Yeah?" She looks up at me, her crystal blue eyes filled with hope.

"Yeah."

Chapter Eleven

Violet

I might be a person who tries my hardest not to lie, but I sure was talking complete and utter bullshit when I told him I had 'heaps of food' at home. My cupboards have never looked so bare.

Inviting him over for dinner was not the best plan I've ever had. I just wasn't ready for our time together to end, so I panicked and threw out the first idea I thought of.

Rylan's sitting in my living room, and he's undoubtedly the best-looking thing that's ever walked through my front door – so even though I have nothing but baked beans to feed him, I still have to admit it was definitely worth the little white lie.

He's made himself at home in here. His shoes are off and his jacket is draped over the back of my couch.

I like it – I like it so much I'm actually having trouble focusing on the problem at hand... the fact that it'll be time to start dinner within an hour, and I have next to nothing here to cook for him.

"What are you planning to have for dinner?" he calls out to me, like he can somehow sense my distress from across the room.

I grimace and glance around, hoping for some type of suggestion to jump out at me.

"Well I know how much you like surprises," I reply coyly as I stall for time.

He laughs and the knot in my stomach eases.

"Do you want some help, Vi?"

He's never called me 'Vi' before, and even though most of the people in my inner circle call me either 'Vi' or 'Letty', it's different when it's coming from him.

It feels like a sign of us growing closer – growing together.

It's enough of a sign for me to take a deep breath and let go of some of my nerves.

This isn't a big deal.

He won't care that I have nothing to feed him – I'm yet to meet a male that has an objection to eating takeout and I doubt he'll be any different.

I just need to relax, stop stressing about things that don't matter and enjoy having him here with me while it lasts.

I'm about to admit my predicament and suggest we order Chinese food when I hear my front door open.

"Knock, knock!" calls the familiar voice from *inside* my house. "We're early."

I bring my hand up to my forehead in disbelief. I can't *believe* I forgot what day of the week it is.

It's pizza night tonight.

Lucy and Emmett, along with my *entire* family come over here for pizza every Sunday night.

"Oh *crap*," I mutter under my breath.

I'm not sure if I'm ready for Rylan to meet my family, or more to the point, for my family to subject him to the rounds of interrogation that they're bound to, but at the same time, I can think of nothing worse than him walking back out of my door so soon after arriving.

Rylan obviously hears the unexpected visitor too because he appears in front of me in the kitchen.

He must see the expression on my face because he chuckles. "You forget you were expecting company?"

I groan. "I'm so sorry. It's Lucy and Emmett... we have dinner every Sunday with my *whole* family... I guess it slipped my mind."

He smiles and steps forward to take my hands in his. He intertwines his fingers with mine and looks down at me with the sweetest expression on his face.

"It's okay... we can do this another night. It's no big deal."

All I can think about is stretching up to kiss him – so I do.

My lips meet his in the way I've been craving all day long. He sighs in satisfaction against my mouth and my legs turn to jelly.

"Ooh la la... hello there, good doctor." Lucy's voice comes from behind me, and the intrusion is enough to break our lips apart, but not our eyes.

The brief yet passionate contact tells me everything I need to know – he's right where he should be and there's no way I'm letting him leave now.

"*Stay*," I whisper to him.

***

I can't recall what I was worried about.

It's almost as though he's been part of Sunday night dinner forever. He fits in so effortlessly that I'm waiting for the moment where the penny drops and it all goes wrong.

Sadly, that's what the circumstance surrounding my life has taught me to expect. But for now, at least, everything seems to be going better than I could have hoped for.

My mum *loves* him. Even if she hadn't cornered me in the kitchen earlier to tell me exactly that, I would have known anyway – it's obvious to see that she's absolutely smitten with him.

Charlie's looking at him with total admiration – like he wants to be him when he grows up. Even Auggie is a fan. She told me, and I quote, that 'he really *is* cute... *and* a doctor too', so as far as August goes, that's praise of the highest kind.

My dad hasn't threatened to shoot him if he hurts me like he did to August's first boyfriend, so that too is a win in my book.

Lucy is sitting in her usual spot, watching the whole thing play out like she's some type of cupid genius. She might be awfully smug that things are working out well so far, but I can also see how genuinely thrilled she is that there's finally a man in my life. I know she's been worried; we probably all have – that I'd never find someone to share myself with.

Sure, it's early days yet, and he might run a mile when I tell him the truth, but this is still so much more promising than any other relationship I've had. It's *progress*. And regardless of the result, it's going to be a good learning curve for me.

There's a chance that meeting my family could even work in my favour – maybe it'll help him to separate me from my condition.

Even Lucy's mum is a little bit in love with him.

I should have realised that they would know each other – Linda has been a nurse in the paediatric ward at Royal West since before I was born.

She, Emmett and Rylan all work in the same place so it's like a little hospital reunion in here.

Linda doesn't join us every Sunday, but I can tell she's awfully chuffed that she decided to attend tonight.

I can't even blame her really, Rylan is more than worth looking at, and when he opens his mouth, he only gets more attractive. He's smart and funny and I can't speak for everyone in the room, but I can't help but be drawn into his presence.

Much to my relief, no one has mentioned my heart – not that they often do on these nights, but still, the worry was there.

Considering this evening was entirely forgotten by me, I couldn't have planned it better if I'd tried.

Lucy's mum and my parents have just left, and my brother and sister are about to follow suit.

Everyone seems a little more reluctant than usual to go and I'm under no illusion that there's a reason other than Rylan that's responsible for their hesitation. He's been a hot commodity at this little get together – he's captured the attention of all of us.

Charlie is chewing his ear off about some surf spot down the coast, and to be honest I don't even know if the man I'm dating knows how to surf or not, but if he doesn't, he's making a really good show of seeming interested in what my younger brother is telling him.

It warms my heart to watch.

August has been quiet tonight, and considering she usually talks more than anybody I've ever met, I'm slightly concerned that she's unwell.

"Auggie."

She's watching our brother and Rylan talking with an inquisitive expression on her face – she doesn't appear to be aware that I've even spoken.

"Auggie."

I break her focus and she looks around, almost as though she's forgotten where she is.

"Huh?"

"Are you alright? You've barely said a word all night."

She shrugs and her gaze flickers back over to Rylan and Charlie before meeting mine. "I'm fine. I guess I'm just curious."

"About Rylan?"

She nods. "He's the man who saved your life…"

Technically it was Dr. White and her team who saved my life that day, but I know what she means – if it weren't for his voice and his eyes, I'm not sure I would have had the strength to hold on and stay.

I hope I get the chance to tell him about it someday – to make him see all that he's done for me before we ever even met.

I hope I get to make sense of it at some point too.

There's no logical explanation as to why it was him I saw, but maybe one day it'll all click into place.

I don't know how it could, but since he came into my life for real, I feel like I don't know anything for certain anymore, other than the fact that *he's* here… and because of him, so am I.

Chapter Twelve

Rylan

"*Stay*," she whispers for the second time this evening.

Blush stains her cheeks as she asks her unspoken question.

"I mean it seems silly... I'm picking you up tomorrow any-way..."

I sweep a strand of hair off her forehead.

I've found myself at her front door once again, the two of us alone under the stars.

Her arms are wrapped around my waist, tugging me tight against her, while one of my hands is resting on the back of her neck, the other cupping her jaw.

I'm not sure I'll ever tire of the feel of her mouth on mine. Even now, we've been apart only thirty seconds or so, and I'm already yearning for more.

"It *does* seem silly," I murmur before brushing my lips ever so softly against hers again.

She sighs, a soft, breathy sound that I'm beginning to really love.

I want to stay, God do I want to stay here with her all night, but I won't – that much I already know.

Not yet.

"Oh wow, I've just realised what I've implied..." Her face somehow manages to go a deeper shade of red. "I'm not talking about sex... I just thought we could sleep next to one another..."

I'm biting back a smile as she stumbles over her words, her nerves blindingly obvious.

"I'm digging myself a hole here; can you say something *please*?"

"Breathe, Violet."

She nibbles on the corner of her lip and forces her eyes to meet mine.

She's so beautiful it pains me – she appeals to me in a way no woman ever has.

I can't put my finger on exactly what it is about her that I find so intriguing, it's not just her eyes, but the stories that they tell and the secrets they keep, it's not just her lips, but the way they move and the seduction they exude. Every feature on her face is not only pretty, but filled with depth, knowledge and power too.

To top it all off, she's got absolutely no comprehension of how stunning she is and that only adds to the appeal of her.

"I know you didn't mean sex." I grin at her, both because I'm amused and because I want her to relax.

I never considered for a second that she would be inviting me up to spend the night with her in that way – things might be moving fast, and I might already like her more than any woman I've ever dated, but neither of us is ready for that yet.

When that time does finally come, I'm going to make sure I do it the right way. I've got a pretty strong hunch that Violet isn't equipped with a whole lot of knowledge on this particular topic, so I want to take things slow.

"And even though I can think of nothing more satisfying than having you fall asleep next to me, I think we should take a rain check, okay?"

"You're such a gentleman," she teases.

I might not have been this way my whole life, but she brings the chivalrous side out in me... she makes me want to say and do things that will sweep her off her feet.

"Can I make a confession?" I ask her.

She nods at me and smiles. Those gorgeous little dimples appear in her cheeks and for a second I can't remember what it was I was planning to confess.

She raises her brows in question.

"These past few days, every moment I'm not with you... I'm wishing I was."

She doesn't say anything, but the huge smile on her face is enough of a reply for me.

She's happy, really happy, and that's when it hits me – If I never achieve another thing in this lifetime, then I would still die a satisfied man.

***

Leaving her just now was the hardest thing I've done in a long time.

Especially after meeting her family – they're what a family should be... loving, warm and welcoming.

I've not been part of a family like that in a long time, but I truly felt as though I was tonight. They welcomed me with open arms and made me feel like I belonged there.

I hope I do belong there – right there with her.

Hanging out with her, Emmett and Lucy had been as easy as breathing. I can picture us as two couples, off in the distant future. We're friends – we're in each other's lives constantly. The minute the image hits my mind I realise just how badly I want exactly that.

I want it all. Her family, her friends, but most importantly, I want *her*.

It would have been so easy to stay... to fall asleep with her in my arms, but I *had* to leave.

I know she's beginning to trust me, I can see it in her eyes. Just the fact that she invited me into her home, let alone her bed tells me that.

But she hasn't found the time to tell me about her heart yet – which means she doesn't trust me entirely.

I'm more than aware it's up to me to earn that trust from her.

Nothing comes free in this world and having faith in a person is probably the biggest testament to that.

She needs to understand I'm in this for a long time, not just a good time, and until she does, I'll be kissing her goodnight at her front door and not between her sheets.

The fact that I was able to do it – that I found it within me to walk away from her when I so effortlessly could have stayed, has given me the strength to do something that I haven't done in a long time.

I know it's kind of creepy to visit a cemetery so late at night, but it's been far too long since I was here, and I have a feeling I won't be able to sleep a wink until I've done this.

I need to talk to my sister, and even though I live in the house she once called home, this is the only place that I seem to be able to feel close to her anymore.

It probably makes me appear crazy – coming to a ghost for advice, but I don't have anywhere else to go.

My father's been gone a long, long time. My mother doesn't even recognise me anymore, and I don't have a lot of friends left.

You spend three years drowning in grief, throwing yourself into your work and pushing people away, and eventually they stay there.

I learnt that the hard way.

There's only so much you can do for someone that doesn't want to help themselves, and while, on the outside, I might have appeared to be together and whole – I've actually been anything but.

Daisy was my rock, my sounding board and my best friend. Losing her destroyed me.

And she might be gone, but I still need her now.

I'd give anything to hear her voice again, even just one more time. I know that I won't get to – that miracles like that don't happen in real life, but it doesn't stop me from wishing for it.

I want to tell her about Violet so badly it hurts.

I know she would have loved her. I don't see how anybody couldn't... she's so pure, and sweet and *good*.

She's so damn easy to love.

The realisation that I'm falling for her doesn't scare me the way that I expected it would. My cold, black heart somehow still beats in rhythm and now it's as though it's beating just for her. Ever since she fell into my orbit I've felt a sense of purpose again.

I smile.

I laugh.

I'm enjoying my life – I'm actually living it.

No longer am I just floating through my days. I'm grounded and I'm *feeling*... I'm feeling things I've never felt before.

I approach the spot where my sister was laid to her final rest and I whisper into the darkness.

"I found her, Daisy... I think I've found the one."

Chapter Thirteen

Violet

"The movies?" He guesses his approximately one hundredth wrong guess.

"Nope." I shake my head. "You really are terrible at this, you know that, right?"

"You mean the aim of the game *isn't* for me to get it repeatedly wrong?"

I haven't told him that I'm only a volunteer at the animal shelter – not a paid employee, so I would imagine that's why he hasn't guessed it's where we're headed.

I'm really nervous about this entire day.

I've decided that today is the day I'm going to tell him about my heart.

I have to – it's time.

I'm starting to feel things for him – *real* things that seem to be boarding the train headed for love.

I don't know how he's feeling about me, but if he's even looking in the same direction as I am, then I need to tell him now before he gets in too deep.

It's not fair to keep him in the dark. Even though life has dealt me a whole series of unfair cards, I still try my hardest to play that hand with respect and dignity – especially where people I care about are concerned, and he's quickly become one of the people on that list.

"Well," he announces. "I'm out of ideas."

I giggle at his perplexed expression. My eyes trace over the curve of his lips as his face breaks into a cheeky grin.

I linger on his blue eyes, the same ones I still picture in my sleep most nights.

My dreams have shifted slightly, where before it was only his eyes and his voice that stayed with me; they've now evolved to include the smile that lights up those eyes, and the warmth of his hand in mine.

The man of my dreams has turned out to be exactly that, and I hope more than anything that he'll still be that man after he learns the truth about me.

"We're here." I grin. "Do you think you might be able to figure it out now?"

He glances around out the window before spotting the sign and laughing – presumably at his own foolishness.

"You're right. I really do suck at this game."

I eye him carefully. "If you'd rather do something else, we can—"

"I can't think of anything else I'd rather do," he cuts me off.

I beam at him. I'm glad he feels that way, because there's nothing I'd rather be doing either.

***

"And this is Smokey, Fluffy and Socks." I point into the enclosure housing three cats, one grey, one ginger and fluffy, and one black with white feet.

He raises his brow at me and smirks. "Original."

I grin. He's not wrong.

"Where did they all come from?" He glances around the large room where we keep all the cats.

I shrug. "Most of them get dumped, some are brought in hurt or unwell, some get taken from their owners... we do our best to fix them up, get them fed and healthy and then find them homes."

He sticks his fingers through one of the gaps and Fluffy rubs up against him.

I can't stop myself from smiling as I watch him scratching under the cat's chin.

There's just something incredibly attractive about a man who's kind to animals.

"Don't you just want to take them all away with you?"

"I have to talk myself out of it every time I leave," I confess.

We stroll past a few more enclosures, heading out towards where they keep the dogs.

There's someone special I want him to meet out there.

"Have you ever given in and taken one home?" He takes my hand in his and swings them between us as he asks.

"Once. I've got a cat, but he hates everyone." I giggle.

He frowns at me. "Why'd you take him then?"

"I dunno. He's just a real grumpy old thing. He hisses if you go near him... he would have been in here forever, and that just made me sad. All he does is sleep all the time, and he eats more than he should, but at least he has a home."

I catch his eye and he's looking at me like I'm something amazing.

I can feel the blush creeping onto my cheeks – it never fails to make an appearance whenever he's around.

I glance over his shoulder and see Avery approaching, and even though I know she's bound to say something that will embarrass me further, I'm so happy that she's here today and she'll get to meet Rylan.

"Hey!" she calls out as she rushes over to us.

I get a half wave and Rylan gets an extended hand. "Hi, I'm Avery, you must be Violet's boyfriend."

The blush I had before is nothing compared to the way my face is flaming now.

"This is Rylan. Rylan, this is my friend Avery," I reply quickly. "Avery is one of the full-time vet nurses here."

I'm hoping to save him from the embarrassment of having to clarify that he's not actually my boyfriend by offering him a piece of information to cling onto.

"I'm Rylan," he confirms as he takes her hand in his. "But between you and me, I like the sound of *Violet's boyfriend* better."

He winks at me and I'm at a loss for words.

The buzzer in Avery's pocket lets out a shrill tone and I'm literally saved by the bell from what was bound to be an awkward interrogation for all involved.

"Gotta go, Violet's boyfriend Rylan." She grins at him and much to my surprise, he grins right back. "It was nice to meet you."

"It was nice to meet you too, Violet's friend Avery."

I don't know precisely what just happened here, but it's making my heart race.

"What?" he questions the perplexed expression I have on my face as I watch her jog off to help out with a new arrival.

"Nothing…" I shake my head.

He looks so happy and carefree; it's a real transformation from the man I met such a short time ago. He's relaxed somewhat and he's more comfortable with me now – he's still got the potential to be intense and smouldering at the drop of a hat, but I like that about him. I actually like it a lot. Being the sole focus of that intensity makes me feel interesting and attractive, and I welcome that feeling.

"She seems nice."

His obvious cheerfulness makes me feel even guiltier for the secrets I'm keeping from him.

I want to be able to call him my boyfriend so badly it almost hurts, but I'm not willing to discuss that label again until he knows what he's getting himself into.

"She is," I agree. "Now come on." I tug on his hand before he can say anything more. "Come say hi to Bear."

Bear is my favourite animal in the whole shelter, and as much as I want him to find a home with people that will love him, I can't imagine this place without him.

"Let me guess, he's big and cuddly?" Rylan drawls.

I don't need to answer, because the dog in question spots me then and comes bounding toward us, all one hundred kilograms of him.

"Bear!" I call to him.

He's so excited to see me, his tail is wagging like crazy as I crouch down to pat and cuddle him.

"When I said big and fluffy, I wasn't imagining it quite to this extreme."

I laugh as Rylan squats down next to me and gets a lick on the face from my best canine friend.

"I think he likes you."

"I like you too, bud, but preferably without your tongue down my throat, huh?" he teases as he scratches the huge St. Bernard on his belly.

"What do you do with him?"

"I normally take him for a walk down to the river..."

I'm not sure how much of his day Rylan was planning to spend in this place with me, but as I watch him with Bear, he certainly doesn't seem in a hurry to get out of here.

"You walk him, or he walks you?" He raises one of his brows at me.

I laugh again, because it's true. I weigh about half of what this big boy does, and if it weren't for the fact that he's decided he's happy to listen to what I say, there's no way I'd be able to make him do anything he didn't want to do.

"It's a bit of both." I giggle.

"How about you pick on someone your own size." He grins at the big dog like they're already best friends.

If I wasn't already falling for this man, I know I would be now.

"Let's go then. Where's his lead, gorgeous?" he asks me over his shoulder.

I don't know if I'm more thrilled that he wants to come with us, or that he called me gorgeous, but either way, I don't speak, I just smile and point.

***

"Urgh, *Bear*!" I cry as he shakes the water out of his long coat right in front of where Rylan and I are seated as we throw sticks into the river for him to fetch.

"Get it, boy." Rylan sends another stick flying into the cool river and Bear bounds off after it.

I smile as I watch him leap in with a splash.

"I've gotta ask... why don't you adopt him? It's obvious you love him."

I've been waiting for this question from him ever since I introduced him to Bear.

There are a few reasons, but I still haven't found the nerve to tell him about my heart, so for now I decide to start with the easiest excuse to explain.

"My place isn't fenced, it'd be no good for him."

I realise just how lame it sounds the moment I say it out loud.

"So build a fence?"

"I'm not exactly known for my construction skills."

He raises a brow at me as though he knows I'm full of crap.

He's right too. If that was all there was to it I would have had the section fenced the moment Bear got brought in to us.

I'd love a dog to keep me company in the big house I call home, but I know I can't take care of him the way he deserves. He'd need walking every day, and if it's too cold for me to go out, or too wet, then Bear would be stuck at home with me instead of getting the exercise he needs.

Then there's my life expectancy, I'm more confident these days, but I've lived with fear in the back of my mind for the past three years that my body would reject my new heart and I'd drop dead.

Bear is only two years old, he's still got a lot of life ahead of him and it wouldn't be fair of me to take him on when I'm not sure I could outlive him.

I try to live my life to the fullest and make the most of the second chance I've been given, and a huge part of me wants to take him home for that very reason alone, but it wouldn't be fair of me – and I can't imagine making such a selfish choice.

I don't realise that I've fallen silent as I watch Bear swimming out towards the stick.

When I look up, Rylan's eyes are watching me intensely, seeing things I'm not sure how to find the courage to explain.

"What's the real problem, Violet?" He asks the question in a soft voice, but there's a hoarse edge to his tone, like he's sensed that bad news is coming his way.

This is it. This is my make or break moment.

I know what I need to do, this is as good of a time as any and I *have* to do this now. I've just got to, as Lucy so diplomatically puts it, 'find my lady balls'.

"There's something I haven't told you." I whisper the words, but he hears me, I know he does.

His eyes never leave mine as he gives me a look that indicates I should carry on.

"I know I should have told you sooner, but I didn't know what *this* was..." I indicate between the two of us. "I promise I was never trying to deceive you." My voice is louder now, but I'm almost shaking with nerves.

"Violet," he murmurs as he takes my hand in his. "Just take a deep breath and say what you need to say."

"It's a long story," I warn.

"I've got nowhere else to be."

I search his eyes for a hint that he'll run – that what I'm about to tell him might scare him off, but I find nothing to confirm my fears, all I see looking back at me is a tender gaze.

"Tell me," he whispers, his voice sounding like gravel.

So I do.

I tell him about the condition I was born with. I tell him about the surgeries and all the hospital stays. I tell him about my heart transplant and the medication that I take each morning. I tell him why I can't take Bear home with me and what I live with every single day.

I tell him everything except for the part where I nearly didn't make it – I don't tell him about seeing his eyes or hearing his voice. I'm not ready to share that with him yet. If he sticks around after this, which I can't possibly imagine he will, then maybe one day I'll find the courage to confide in him about that too.

When I finally finish spewing out my life story, I'm out of breath. I don't know how long I've been talking for, but Bear is out of the river now and has lay down in the sun to dry... and Rylan, he's still staring at me with the same tender expression he was when I started speaking.

There's no pity in his eyes, there's no anger, resentment or disappointment there either. In fact, if anything, he looks relieved, and I have to wonder if he's known all along that there's something I've been keeping from him.

He's an incredibly insightful man, and it's a possibility I can't discount.

"I'm sorry I didn't tell you sooner, but I just wanted to feel... *normal*, I guess... I wanted to be the woman falling in love with the man for just a little while longer before my heart got in the way."

He's doesn't say a word, just reaches out with his free hand and tentatively places his palm against the spot where my heart beats.

I thought he'd have questions, accusations perhaps... but he's silent. I don't know what this means, but I allow myself to enjoy the moment of what feels a lot like wordless acceptance.

"I can feel it beating."

I don't recall closing my eyes, but upon hearing his whispered voice, my lids flutter open again.

I don't reply, I'm waiting for something, *anything* more from him.

I need him to respond – to tell me that I shouldn't have kept this from him... to tell me that he doesn't want to be with the girl with the broken heart.

He slowly pulls away his hand, and I watch the movement with a fierce intensity.

He's bound to talk now, he *has* to. There's got to be something he wants to say to me.

I'm waiting for it, so when he does finally speak I don't anticipate being taken by surprise by the words he chooses.

"You're falling for me?"

It's the last thing I expect him to say. In fact, it's not until he asks the question that I realise I said those words aloud to him. I was so caught up in my story, in my heart... that I didn't even acknowledge what I was admitting.

I consider denying it, but I don't know what the point would be in that. I've laid out almost all my cards and there's no reason I can think of that I should hide the truth from him.

I can only control *me*, and right now, I want him to know exactly how I feel about him.

"I am... I'm falling in love with you."

His answering smile is so blinding I literally have to look away.

He's ecstatic, and I'm confused.

He reaches for my jaw and runs his thumb gently down the skin on my cheek as he tilts my gaze back up to meet his.

His stare is so intense; I feel it all the way down to my toes.

He leans in so our faces are only an inch apart. "I'm right here falling with you," he whispers before pressing his lips against mine.

Chapter Fourteen

Rylan

It's so much worse than I imagined, but at the same time, it's better too.

Violet has been to hell and back, *repeatedly*, but she's still here… living and breathing… she's *alive*.

She's a fighter and I believe she's already made it through the worst of what life will throw at her.

Looking at her, such a bright, beautiful woman, you'd never guess the horrors she's endured – the opponents she's taken on and won.

There are already so many things I can think of that I want to ask her in regards to what she's been through, but I don't.

There will be plenty of time for that later. I'm not going anywhere and if I have my way, neither will she.

I'm in this for the long haul, and if she thinks that her heart is going to make a difference to the way I feel about her, then she's going to have to think again.

The only thing I need to know about her heart right now is that I hold a piece of it.

I can tell she's worried, and I've got a feeling she's expecting me to walk away. I don't blame her for her insecurity surrounding what she's just shared with me. I can't even begin to imagine everything she's been through. It literally brings a tear to my eye to imagine that she must feel that way for a reason – that people must have steered clear of her in the past due to something she has not an ounce of control over.

I've had people avoid me too – leave me all alone, so I sort of understand what it's like... but I also know that's on me – I didn't give anyone a reason to stay. Violet gives people all the reasons in the world.

I may not have known her for a huge amount of time, but it didn't take long to figure out what kind of a person she is.

She's open, kind, strong, warm and loving... I know I'm not the first person to feel this kind of love from Violet, but I think that maybe I might be the only man whom she's not related to that's ever been allowed to get this close, and that's not an honour I'll take lightly.

Her lips are still on mine and she's kissing me back with the fervour of someone who might never get another chance.

That's when it hits me that it's probably *exactly* the way she feels.

She's just laid everything out bare for me – literally put her heart on the line and I haven't said a word about it.

I undoubtedly know it changes nothing about the way I feel for her, but *she* doesn't know that yet.

I pull back, breaking our kiss but she's not done, she has the front of my shirt fisted in her hand and it pains me to think she's holding on for dear life.

"Violet," I murmur against her lips as she kisses me again.

Her breath is heavy as she releases me before resting her forehead against mine.

Her eyelids are flickering open and shut and it takes me a moment to recognise that she's crying.

"I'm here," I whisper. I wrap my arms around her and pull her onto my lap.

I wrap my arms around her like a vice as she clings onto my neck and shoulders.

Her small frame is wracked with sob after sob, and I just hold her as tight as I can.

As much as it pains me to see her upset, I don't bother telling her not to cry. There would be no point... she needs this release and after all I've just heard, she deserves a good cry.

She deserves a lot of things, and I'm going to do everything in my power to give her all I have to offer.

Bear wanders over and nudges Violet with his head. It's a small gesture, but it warms my insides.

She's like a magnet; it's not only me she's pulled in, but this big dog too.

She reaches out and strokes his head and reassures him that she's okay, that she *will* be okay.

He curls up at our feet and I smile.

Violet's sobs have subsided, and she turns in my arms so she can look up at me.

"I'm sorry."

"You don't have to apologise for being human."

"I got your shirt all wet."

"I think I can live with that."

She's looking up at me with her big crystal blue eyes, and even though they're brimmed with tears, I've never seen her look so beautiful.

She's staring at me, searching for answers that it doesn't appear she's finding.

"Why aren't you running?" she finally whispers.

I reach my hand forward and wipe away a stray tear from her cheek.

"I'm not going anywhere."

"But aren't you worried... don't you have questions?"

I nod. "I have questions, but they can wait... I'm not going anywhere, and no answer you could give would change how I feel about you anyway."

She opens her mouth to speak but no words come out, so I continue.

"And as for being worried... truthfully, I *am*."

She sighs in defeat, like maybe this is the 'but' moment she's been dreading.

"I'm worried that I'll lose you, and I don't mean because of your heart... I mean because of your head. I'm worried you'll convince yourself this isn't a good idea and you'll leave me."

Her chin lifts slowly until she's looking into my eyes and I see the deep-seated fear she usually keeps hidden there.

She's scared, and rightfully so, but she doesn't have to be scared on her own anymore.

Sure, she's got her family and friends, but until now she's never had me, and I'm willing to do whatever it takes to make her happy. I know I can't make the things she fears disappear, but I can share the load with her – I can lighten the weight on her shoulders, if nothing else.

"I worry about letting people in... it hurts me to think what will happen to those closest to me if I die."

She may have just told me all of the facts about her heart, and shared with me some of her most tightly kept secrets, but this right here is possibly the truest thing of all to fall from her lips.

Her biggest fear of death isn't for herself, but for those she'll leave behind.

That one sentence sums up exactly what type of person she is, and I fall a little bit further down the rabbit hole of love because of it.

She's got to be the most selfless person I've ever met.

I make a vow to myself that I'll never be someone she can push away, that I'll never let her see herself as a burden to me, because she isn't.

I know her fears are justified, and there's no point in telling her otherwise, because she's right – loving her carries the risk of losing her, but there's one thing I know for absolute certain in all this, and it's that this is a risk I'm willing to take.

Bear might not have a choice about whether or not he goes home with Violet, but I sure as hell do, and I'm not going to let her go without a fight – and if I'm honest, probably not even then.

Chapter Fifteen

Violet

"So you really like this boy, then?"

The unexpected voice sends me jumping in the air.

"Jesus, Mum, you scared me… what are you doing in here? Is everything okay?"

She's sitting in my living room, making herself at home on one of my couches.

It's not that she's not welcome, but she's never done this before – I've never come home to her alone in here like some type of creeper.

"Everything's fine. I was just waiting for you to get back from your date."

"*Why?* Why didn't you call? How long have you been here for?"

I strip off my jacket and toss it over the back of the seat before joining her on the couch.

"I haven't been here long, and I'm sorry, I shouldn't have just let myself in like that."

I've never been particularly concerned about boundaries with my mum before this point in time, other than with my paintings that is, but now that I have a real life boyfriend and

I'm not a child anymore, I'm suddenly hit with the desire for privacy.

My phone chimes in my pocket with an incoming message and I can't pull it out fast enough. I already know it's Rylan. He's like a drug to me, and even though I don't need him like I need my anti-rejection pills and my other daily dose of medication, I can feel myself beginning to rely on him like he's keeping me alive the very same way.

To: Violet

From: Rylan

Ever since you left I've been trying to convince myself I don't miss you already.

It's not working.

I can't help the smile that spreads wide across my face as I read his words. I've momentarily forgotten all about my mum sitting only an arm's length away, but she hasn't forgotten about me it would seem.

"Well that answers my question about you and that boy then, doesn't it?"

As I sit the phone down I can feel myself blushing. "I'm not sure he should be classed as a boy, Mum. A *man* might be more appropriate."

She raises her brows at me and I realise that I've just insinuated that I'm familiar with his manhood.

I cover my eyes as I feel my face flaming even deeper red.

Mum laughs at my predicament.

"Not like that! You know what I mean... he's not a kid, oh God, this is so embarrassing."

"So... he seems very nice," she prompts me for more information, clearly not yet having got what she's after from this little talk.

"He is, and *yes*, I do like him... I like him a lot actually."

I don't know where she's planning to go with this conversation, but just in case she's about to give me the birds and bees talk, I decide to get in first.

"I know I've never had a real boyfriend, but I'm not fifteen anymore, okay? I'm a grown woman and I can take care of myself."

She nods her head in acceptance, but I can't help but feel a little guilty that she's missed out on that particular milestone with me.

It's a mother's rite of passage to stress about their daughter getting drunk and winding up pregnant, but that was never going to be an issue for me. She more than got her money's worth with Auggie however, so I guess it all evened out in the end.

"I just worry about you."

She's always worried about me and she probably always will, but at some point she's going to have to let go and let me live the life she's fought so hard for me to have.

"I know you do, but I'm fine, really I am. He's a good man."

"Does he know about your heart?"

I nod, and it feels so incredible to be able to answer that question with an honest yes.

"I told him today... it was like I'd confessed something as trivial as the colour of my eyes." I huff out a laugh of disbelief. "Must be the doctor in him."

Mum smiles at me in a knowing way and I instantly feel like a little girl who still has so much to learn.

"I've seen the way he looks at you, Vi, and it's got nothing to do with the fact that he's a doctor." She shrugs. "He's in love with you."

The way she says it, like it's totally straightforward and un-complicated makes the heart in my chest gallop like a race horse.

I might be too old for the safe sex lecture, but I'm not too old to talk to my mum about the new man in my life, so I do.

I tell her everything about him and by the end of it, I'm well aware that I'm in love with him too.

***

He might not have asked me anything much when I first told him about my heart, but he's certainly making up for it now.

He wants to know *everything*.

Only, the questions he's firing at me aren't the ones I expected to hear.

He doesn't seem to want to know about my illness so much as he does my life – he wants to know what I've done with my new heart these past three years.

So I tell him.

"Before my transplant I was studying business."

He raises his brows at me in surprise.

"Mmm hmm." I nod. "I don't know what I was thinking... I dropped it as soon as I was well enough to convince Mum I'd thought it through."

"What did you change to?"

"I didn't…" I shake my head. "I decided that I wanted to explore my real passion."

"Painting." He nods in understanding.

It probably should surprise me that he got the answer correct in one, but it doesn't. He sees *me*, and even though he hasn't seen any of my work – he already seems to know it's important to me.

"I signed up to some local art classes and some short courses. I've done painting, photography, drawing, sculpture, design… you name it, I've probably taken a class."

I taught a few painting classes too, but I decide to leave that part out. This conversation is teetering on the edge of dangerous territory as it is, the last thing I want to do is encourage him to ask to see my work for himself – because I'm not sure I'd have it in me to say no.

"I could have studied art and gotten myself a degree, but what would be the point? I don't need a degree to paint."

He's smiling at me like he agrees with my logic.

"So when you're not working at the shelter, you're painting?"

I crinkle my nose sheepishly. "So, I don't actually work there… I'm a volunteer."

"Huh… that's cool. Do you volunteer anywhere else?"

"Sometimes I hang out with the Heart Kids group I used to be a part of, but that's about it. I'd love to spend some time in the children's ward at the hospital, because I spent so much time in there when I was little, but I can't. My immune system isn't what it should be. Animals have a lot less I can catch."

I don't go into details about the medication I take and how it suppresses my immune system in order to reduce the risk of my body rejecting my new heart – he's a doctor and he probably understands my condition better than I ever could anyway.

That's when the thought occurs to me. He delivers babies, and the defect I have – I was born with. Someone like him probably brought me into the world.

"Have you ever delivered a baby with a heart condition like mine?"

He looks at me with a pained glance and my stomach flips.

"You have, haven't you?"

"I have."

"The baby didn't survive, did it?"

He shakes his head. "The parents decided against medical intervention."

Tears spring to my eyes and I blink them back fiercely.

That could have been me.

If my parents weren't as strong as they are – not that I think those other parents necessarily made a weak choice – they did what was right for them, but in my mind, the strength is in the fight.

I'm so thankful that my parents chose to fight.

"So, you sell your art?" he questions, no doubt in an attempt to distract me from the current topic of conversation.

I laugh nervously. "*God* no."

That would require people to actually see my paintings.

His expression is confused. "Sorry for the intrusion, but how exactly do you pay the bills?"

He sits down his chocolate milkshake on the table, picks up my strawberry one and brings it up to his lips to suck it through the straw.

This conversation was bound to come up at some point; I knew it would, and it's not that I don't want to tell him, but discussing my financial situation always fills me with a feeling of guilt.

"You remember I told you about my Aunt?"

He nods. "Rita, right? She gave you the ring and the house."

I like that he hasn't forgotten what I told him about the ring around my neck, and I appreciate that he recognises it's just as important to me as the big, beautiful house is.

"That's the one... She also left me money – a lot of it. It's invested well and turns over a pretty solid income, so given my medical situation and the fact that I don't really know what I want to do for a job, I've just been volunteering my time and living off the money she left me, even though I don't feel like I deserve that luxury most of the time."

If it was anyone other than him I'd be expecting a question about just how much money I inherited, but I know he won't ask – he's not that type of guy.

"She must have loved you very much. Why wouldn't you deserve it? She obviously wanted you to have it."

I think about the truth in his words for a minute.

She did love me; she loved me like I was her own daughter. She'd been a big part of my life since the day I was born, and I know all she ever wanted was for me to have a real life. It's a hard pill to swallow that I finally got one, and she's not around to see me enjoy it.

She passed so quickly and unexpectedly, none of us saw it coming or had time to process it. She never even told anyone that she was unwell.

"She knew she was dying. She had everything all mapped out, her money, her assets, letters for us all... even her funeral was planned for us. She didn't even look sick." There's tears pooling in the corners of my eyes and I know it won't be long before one escapes down my cheek.

He reaches out and intertwines his fingers with mine across the top of the table.

"You miss her."

I shake my head. "Well I mean, yeah..." I sniff. "I miss her like crazy, but that's not it. It's the guilt that gets me. She left us a couple of months after I got my new heart. All that time she was unwell and the only thing she worried about was *me* and my family. She was there supporting us when it should have been the other way around."

"I'm sure she had her reasons for that."

I don't doubt that she did – Rita had her reasons for everything, but that doesn't make it any easier for me to accept.

"I just *don't* understand. Why did I get to stay when she had to go? Why was my life deemed more important than hers?" I choke the words out.

He squeezes my hand but says nothing – I think he knows I'm not really looking for an answer to my question.

"In a way it feels like I'm responsible for *two* deaths," I whisper.

"You're not responsible for *any* deaths, Violet."

He pulls on my hand so I look at him. His blue eyes are burning into mine with sincerity.

"I know I didn't kill them, but I benefitted from them dying, Rylan. How is that not the same thing?" My voice cracks as I voice my guilt. "A donor – someone I didn't even know – gave me their heart, their actual *heart*. The very thing that keeps us alive was taken from their body and put into mine. I can literally feel another person's heart beating in my chest."

"I'm not going to pretend to understand how it feels to live because somebody else died, because I don't, but I *do* know that none of this is your fault – you didn't ask to be born with this condition, Violet. This isn't on you."

He makes a valid point, but it's still something I have a hard time getting my head around.

"I know they were going to die anyway, and that I needed this organ to live, but it's just so conflicting to think about."

He gives me a sad smile.

"And Rita, she gave me *so* much – she's not just given me money and a roof over my head, she's given me freedom. She gave me the means to do everything I ever wanted... she's the reason I got to travel the world."

"You travelled?"

I nod and smile. "I saw *everything* I've ever wanted to see." I rest my hand over the spot where my heart it. "When I was stuck in the hospital, I promised myself if I ever got a second chance to live, that I'd tick off all of the boxes on my list, so when I got my new heart, that's what I did."

I'm not sure if he's grateful for the change of subject, or if the sights of the world is something that gets him excited, but his face breaks into a smile and his eyes light up.

"Tell me."

"Lucy, Emmett and I went for six months; and Charlie joined us for a month over his summer break."

I sigh as I think about all the incredible places I went and all the amazing things I saw.

"I saw the Louvre and the Mona Lisa in Paris, the Sistine Chapel in the Vatican City, Michelangelo's David in Florence, Banksy in London, The Colosseum in Rome... we went to Vienna, Venice, New York, Barcelona, Mexico, Istanbul, Athens... if it had art, I saw it."

"I think she would have been happy to give you that, Vi. She didn't leave you all of that because she wanted you to feel guilty, she gave it to you so you could live."

He squeezes my hand and I can't help but smile in agreement.

"I think the only reason you'd have to feel guilty is if you weren't doing exactly that."

Chapter Sixteen

Rylan

I wince as the giant dog bounds around my small living room, he knocks into a shelf and sends books flying all over the place.

"*Bear!*" I groan.

It wasn't until I got him in here in this confined space that I realised just how big of a dog he really is.

I didn't even bother to ask if he was full grown yet or not – but he damn well better be, or we're going to have some serious problems with this new arrangement.

He leaps up onto the couch and begins to make himself comfortable in my favourite spot.

I swing open the double doors that lead out to the back yard.

The house might be small, but the yard is huge, and I'm hoping he'll decide that his time is better spent running around out there than it is in here.

"Out you go, boy," I call.

He looks up at me and doesn't budge an inch – we're clearly going to have to work on the command training. It seems the only person the big guy is willing to listen to is Violet, and she's not here, nor does she know of my hare-brained scheme to surprise her, so I'm going to have to find another way to get him to do what I want.

I grab one of the tennis balls off the table and suddenly I have his attention, I throw it out the door onto the grass and he damn near bowls me over chasing after it.

I shut the door behind him, just in case, but it seems he's been distracted from his reign of terror by the scents around the yard and all the objects that need peeing on.

I'll be the first to admit that I didn't think this through particularly thoroughly, but even though he's turned my house upside down in a matter of minutes, I still can't bring myself to regret my decision.

I couldn't stop thinking about the look on Violet's face when we said goodbye to Bear last week. She was heartbroken. She knew as well as I did that a beautiful dog like that wasn't going to stick around an animal shelter forever.

Losing him would have broken her and I couldn't let that happen. Violet's had more breaks in her heart than anyone I've ever met, and I couldn't allow her to endure yet another crack.

Bear had a rough start to life, but thanks to Violet and the other staff at the shelter, he's been nursed back to health, he's put on some weight and he's ready to enjoy himself.

He and Violet have that in common, they've both been dealt a harsh hand in life, but they've both come out stronger for it.

Maybe that's why Bear chose her.

Maybe that's why I chose her too... maybe I need her passion for life to inspire me to do better – to *be* better. Maybe it's time I came out stronger too.

If Violet can live through everything she has and still come out of it with a smile on her face, then I don't think I have a choice than to believe that anything is possible.

I glance back out the window and see that Bear has moved on from peeing on everything and has now begun the process of digging up every plant in my small garden.

I can't even be mad – that dog makes her happy, and seeing her smile is going to be more than worth the mess.

I glance at the time on my watch.

It's my day off, and Violet is about to start working a shift at the shelter for the next five hours, which means I need to get my ass into gear.

I've got a fence to build.

***

I glance around at the progress we're making. I have to stop working for a moment to stop myself from getting all choked up about the support around me.

I know they're all here for Violet, and not for me, but I guess it's just been so long since I felt like I was truly a part of something bigger.

I haven't felt like I've had people I could call on for a favour, for years, but it seems I do now.

Emmett didn't hesitate to agree to help me out and he didn't miss a beat before asking Charlie and Shaun to chip in too.

Even Leanne turned up to get her hands dirty, although I think she's possibly got an ulterior motive for being here.

She wants to know if I care about her daughter. She needs to know that she can trust me with her.

She hasn't said those words, but I can read the woman like a book. She wears her worries on her sleeve and her concerns might as well be tattooed across her forehead.

I don't blame her. Violet might have got a raw deal in life, but I can't even begin to understand the things that Leanne and Shaun went through as her parents. It seems like an impossible situation to imagine, let alone witness those things happening to your own flesh and blood.

I can understand why she's protective of her daughter, and it's up to me to prove that I'm here to stay and that I'd never intentionally do *anything* to hurt Violet.

It's *my* responsibility to show her that I'm capable of taking on the role of protector – not that Violet seems to need it, but I think that perhaps Leanne does… I think that maybe she might need to know that someone is there for Violet, or maybe it's just a matter of having someone to share the worry with.

Whatever it is, I'm putting my hand up for it – I'm *all* in, and I'm hoping that this plan I've put in motion is the first step to proving exactly that to Violet *and* her family.

Violet and I have spoken every single day since her confession by the river. When we haven't been together in person, we've spent countless hours on the phone and every single minute I've spent with her on the other end of the line has had me falling deeper and deeper.

She's a complex creature with so many layers to unwrap and decipher. She's like a puzzle you think you've got all figured out, but then you realise there's a piece hidden under the rug you're yet to even see.

It's what I've decided I love most about her, because it's more than clear to me now that I do love her.

It's why I'm here – why we're all here. We may all be very different people, but we each have one thing in common – *Violet*.

***

We've still got a lot of work to do, but it's a start, and hopefully it's enough of a gesture to show Violet that I'm in this with her for good.

I know she'll be due back soon, and she's bound to be upset over Bear being gone.

I feel bad about convincing Avery it was a good idea to lie to her, but I wanted to show Violet this in private.

Bear spots a bird in the far corner and takes off in an attempt to catch it.

He loves it our here in Violet's newly fenced back yard, and much to my disbelief, he's not dug up a single one of her plants or peed on any of her outdoor furniture.

We've still got the entire front yard to fence, but it's something at least, and it'll give Bear somewhere safe to run around for now.

"I can sort that later," I call to Shaun and Charlie as they restack the leftover timber against the side of the house.

They both proceed to ignore me and carry on doing what they're doing. They've done so much for me already and I feel guilty for hijacking their Saturday the way I have.

Even Lucy is here now. She's far too pregnant to do any type of lifting or building, but she's kept the snacks and drinks flowing for us while we work.

I can feel her watching me – she's been doing it for a while now, and I know sooner or later I'm going to have to hear whatever it is she's planning to say to me.

Violet must be due back any minute, so I decide that now is as good of a time as any.

"Just the man I've been waiting for." She confirms my suspicion as I sit down next to her on the garden bench.

"At your service."

She glances around at our day's work, her eyes lingering a little longer on Emmett than anyone else as she takes her slow appraisal.

"This is going to mean a lot to her," she finally says.

"I hope so."

"*You* mean a lot to her."

I know I do. There's no denying the love in Violet's eyes when she looks at me, and I wouldn't dream of disagreeing with what Lucy said, even if I weren't able to see the truth for myself. She knows Violet better than I do.

"She means a lot to me too."

"I can see that."

Her gaze strays from the yard and lands on my face. She smiles at me.

"I guess you're expecting the speech where I threaten to hunt you down and kill you if you hurt her, right?"

The thought had crossed my mind.

"You should know I don't assume anything when it comes to pregnant women." I chuckle.

"You're a wise man, Dr. Wilder." She grins. "I'll admit, I've been thinking about the little talk you and I would have... but after this I'm not sure you need to hear it."

"I won't hurt her, Lucy."

She smiles at me again. "I know you won't. You adopted a giant freaking dog just to make her smile – I think we're good here."

I laugh as the dog in question leaps up at Leanne, slobbering all down the side of her face as she laughs.

I might have got him with Violet in mind, but truthfully, I kind of like having him around too. He's just another thing I have to thank Violet for. Lucy too – it's because of her that this whole thing began.

"I never got a chance to thank you."

She looks at me quizzically. "For what?"

"For forcing me to agree to that blind date... for *Violet*... for all of it."

"That smile on her face is all the thanks I need."

Lucy's looking past me; back up at the house and when I turn, I see the very smile she's referring to.

Violet's hand flies up to her mouth as her eyes land first on Bear, and then on me as she realises what's going on.

"That's your cue to get over there." Lucy shoves my shoulder and I stumble to my feet.

I don't even make it halfway across the lawn before Violet flies down the steps and throws herself into my waiting arms.

Bear chases after her, leaping and barking in excitement as he goes.

"*You* adopted Bear?" She's staring up at me, her bloodshot eyes wide in bewilderment.

"Surprise." I shrug.

"You built me a fence?" Her voice is beginning to crack and I know it won't be long before the tears start to fall.

"I can't take all the credit for that. I had some help."

I glance around and it's only then that I notice we're alone out here.

They've all left us to enjoy our moment in private.

"I can't believe you did all this for me."

I shrug again. "You love him," I reply simply, because it's the only explanation I'll ever need.

She blinks back the moisture pooling in her eyes and smiles the sweetest smile at me.

"I love *you*."

The earth might technically still be spinning, but *my* whole world has just stopped.

I know there will never be another moment quite like this one. I hope to hear those words from her for a very long time yet, but I can't imagine anything possibly comparing to this first time.

Now I'm the one with teary eyes.

"I love you too." I choke out the words as best I can.

She presses up onto the tips of her toes and I meet her for a kiss. It's so much more passionate than any we've shared before.

I may have spent all day building a fence, but now I can physically feel a wall crumbling down between us.

She's giving me another little piece of herself and I lock it away safely in my heart.

"Thank you," she whispers hoarsely against my lips.

I could say so many things to her right now, I could tell her that I'm crazy about her, that I'm *hers*... that I can't manage to picture my life without her in it anymore. I could tell her that I think she's had my heart from the moment I first laid eyes on her, but instead I just hold her tight and soak up some more of her light.

Chapter Seventeen

Violet

There's not a lot of things I've allowed myself to have in the past twenty-five years.

There's my passion for painting and there's my friendship with Lucy, but outside of my favourite hobby and my best friend, I've made a real effort not to take anything more from the universe – in a lot of ways I feel like I've already taken enough.

I know I'm not responsible for the loss of a life, but I benefited from one and it often feels like the same thing.

So I try not to take. Instead I do my best to *give*.

But now, here in this moment, as I see the deep, unwavering love in his eyes, I know I have to allow myself this.

I have to allow myself *him*.

I'm entitled to live and love, just like everyone else is, and I have to give this everything I have, even though I know I'm going to receive so much more back in return.

Rylan is here in front of me, figuratively naked, baring his soul to me.

He sees *me*. The *real* me.

My borrowed heart is so tangled up with his, it's like they're one and the same – that it seems like they're beating together.

It's just the two of us and Bear in my big house, but I've never felt less alone. He's everywhere I look. I can feel him all around me and I can smell his scent in the air.

He lets go of me and tugs his t-shirt slowly over his head. The sight is so perfect it seems too good to be true. His golden skin stretches flawlessly over his tight, toned muscles and there's not a mark out of place.

My head is screaming at me that he's too good for me – that I couldn't possibly deserve someone this faultless, but the look in his eyes quietens my silent objection.

He reaches for my hand and ever so slowly lifts it to the spot on his chest where I can feel his heart beating. My hand rests there as he mirrors the action, placing his own hand over my heart.

I can feel the steady thrum of his heart and know that he's experiencing the same.

I fill my lungs deeply and as I release my breath, I let my hand wander over his chest and across the grooves of his abdomen. I feel him shudder under my touch and I revel in the reaction I've evoked.

"*Violet*," he whispers as he dips his head and his mouth briefly comes into contact with mine.

There have been plenty of times when I've felt nervous in my life; I can think of half a dozen that spring to mind in an instant, and they're *all* to do with my heart.

This is too, but not in the same way.

This is something new.

This is about what my heart *wants*, not what it needs for once, and all that my heart wants in this moment, is *him*.

"I've never done this before," I whisper back as he places soft kisses along my collar bone.

He pauses and looks up at me. "Never?"

He doesn't seem shocked – maybe a bit surprised, like perhaps I've just confirmed a lucky guess.

I shake my head no.

No one has ever wanted me the way Rylan does. No man has ever got to know the real me like he has.

"I'm broken goods."

I'm embarrassed that I'm still a virgin at twenty-five years old, but there's also a small part of me that's glad, I may not have known I was saving myself for him, but it sure feels that way now.

I can't think of a better man to share this first with.

"We're all a little bit damaged, Violet." He looks right into my eyes as he speaks.

I like that he doesn't argue with me about it, or try to deny the obvious.

This is one of the things I love the most about him, he doesn't lie to me and he doesn't try to make me feel better by filling me up with untruths. He simply reminds me that I'm not alone – that we all have our flaws, we all have a story... he reminds me to forget the rest.

He kisses me on the skin just below my ear and the sensation is so sharp it feels like broken glass.

I've never been kissed like this before.

He wants *me*, in all the ways a man wants a woman. It's pure desire and primal instincts that are driving him to me.

I want this so badly I can hardly think straight, but I'm still afraid of what he'll think when he sees *every* part of me. I feel like the shy little girl in the changing rooms at school all over again.

My scars aren't red and angry looking like they once were, they've healed and faded somewhat, but for him – seeing them for the first time, it's bound to be a shock.

He tugs on the hem of my shirt, pulling it from the band of the denim shorts I'm wearing.

"Leave it on." I can't stop myself whispering.

It's my shield – my last line of defence, and if he takes that away, he'll never be able to unsee what's beneath it.

He pauses and lets go of the fabric before tipping my chin up so I'm looking right at him.

"You can't hide from me."

"But—"

He shakes his head. "There is *nothing* you need to hide from me, Violet, I see *you*."

He's right... I *know* he's right. I want this with him and I know I can't stay hidden forever – not if I want this to work, and I do... more than I want anything else.

I nod, just one small movement.

Ever so slowly he reaches for my shirt again and one by one unfastens the buttons until it's hanging open in the front.

His eyes are no longer on my face, but on my body now, and the weight of his stare threatens to make my knees buckle.

His strong hands slide the fabric off my shoulders and I watch as it falls to the floor and lands at my feet.

I've never felt this entirely exposed to a person. I know full well I have been – rooms full of doctors have looked at my body in far less than what I'm wearing now, but this is different.

He's not a professional who is looking at me as a patient.

He's just a man who is looking at me as a woman.

I gasp as his fingers run ever so gently over my scar.

"*This* is what you were worried about?" His voice is raw, it sounds like sandpaper.

I nod – I can't speak. It's taking everything I have just to breathe as he exposes more of my secrets one by one.

"You really think I'd scare that easily?"

He doesn't wait for an answer; instead he leans in and kisses my collar bone again, before moving lower and kissing the very spot where the heart I was born with vacated my body.

"Let me help put you back together, Violet."

They're the exact words I need to hear in this moment.

I almost feel stupid for worrying the way I did. I should have known that he wouldn't run... that he wouldn't care about something as superficial as the marks on my skin.

"Rylan," I whisper.

"I'll *never* leave," he whispers back and I feel his lips move against me. "I might need you to put me back together too."

He hears my unspoken fears and soothes them instantly.

I run my hand down his bare front until I reach the waistband of his jeans.

I'm scared, *so* scared, I think I might be more afraid of doing this than I've ever been of anything that came before it, but I take that leap, because it's not just some guy in front of me.

It's *Rylan*.

I love him, and he loves me back – every last broken bit of me.

Chapter Eighteen

Rylan

I can't recall us having the conversation, but it seems something unspoken has passed between us this past month.

I haven't spent more than twelve hours away from Violet since the night she gave me another of her firsts.

We're joined now – bound in a way I can't even begin to understand.

I'm not the same man I was a few months ago. He's still there, deep inside me, but he's evolved somewhat.

I no longer live and breathe my job – I still love what I do, but for the first time ever, I love something else more.

I love *her* more.

I love her more than I love anything else in my life.

She makes my pulse speed up and time slow down.

Our two separate paths have been diverted to flow alongside each other almost effortlessly.

It seems too easy most of the time – we fit together so naturally that it almost seems too good to be true.

We laugh and play, we watch movies and talk about books, we take Bear for walks and lie out under the stars, we discuss everything from politics to fan fiction theories and cook to-gether nearly every day.

I don't have to worry about missing out on time with her because of my job – she's more than comfortable adjusting to the long shifts and erratic callouts. When I work, Violet paints or volunteers and when we sleep we do it together.

Painting, I'm beginning to learn, is Violet's escape from the world.

Sometimes my phone rings in the middle of the night, and when I return to her place, there's a jar of dirty brushes sitting in the sink.

I don't know if she paints to fill the time that I'm gone, or if she paints *because* I'm gone.

She's never offered to show me her work, and I know her well enough to know that it's not a slip of her mind.

She's not ready to show me yet and I can respect that for now.

There's things I'm not ready to share with her yet either – things like my sister.

Every now and then something will happen and the pain of losing her hits me like a slap to the face.

Today was one of those days.

An old friend of Daisy's – a nurse that had worked with her, came back from overseas this week. She didn't do anything wrong, but she obviously didn't get the memo that all my other colleagues did.

She talked about Daisy, she laughed and reminisced about the good times they'd had together.

I know that's how it should be – that years after someone's gone you *should* be able to talk about them, but it doesn't seem to work that way for me.

Where others seem to light up at an old memory, I feel like I'm being filled with lead, and I'm about to be dropped into dark, murky water with no way out.

It's moments like these that I feel most lost and alone. Only I'm *not* alone anymore.

I've got Violet, and right now I need her more than I ever have.

***

I arrive back to a sight that steals all of the breath from my lungs.

Violet is sprawled on her couch, Bear on the floor next to her. She's sketching in a book that I've never been allowed to look in and she's dressed in tracksuit bottoms and a tank top – the type of top that *doesn't* cover the marks on her chest.

I know her scars still bother her, but this small step where she's chosen not to cover up feels like huge progress in my mission to assure her that I don't see her for her struggles.

As much as I want to celebrate this incredible milestone, I'm so emotionally spent that I don't think I can manage anything more than to hold her close.

She'll make everything better just like she always does.

She hears me come in and there's already a smile on her lips before she even raises her gaze to meet mine.

I'm not sure what she sees when she looks at me, but judging by the look on her face, it can't be anything good.

"Rylan." She scrambles up off the couch and the normally treasured sketch pad falls to the ground with a thud.

She doesn't say another word until she's in my arms.

"What is it?"

I want to tell her, I *do*, but I don't know how. I can't figure out how to make my mouth open so the words can come out.

I try, over and over, but nothing happens, so I give up trying.

Instead, I bury my face in her hair and just breathe. Each breath is more calming than the next and I find the tight coil inside my gut loosening with each fill of my lungs.

She's gripping me tight, like she can't get close enough.

I hoist her up and she clamps her legs around my waist, her arms are wrapped firmly around my neck, holding me as close to her as I possibly can be.

When I'm here like this, with her in my arms, the thought of talking about my sister doesn't seem so life shattering anymore – I can't help but consider the possibility that I could do *anything* as long as Violet was right there with me.

"Rylan?" she whispers after what feels like forever.

"I'm okay..."

"Do you want to talk about it?"

As much as I want to tell her yes, I can't right now, I'm dead on my feet and I know I'll need every ounce of strength to share my story with her.

"Could we just go to bed?"

"If that's what you need," she replies softly.

"I just need *you*."

"You've got me, Rylan."

Chapter Nineteen

Violet

I clutch my chest and drag in a deep breath.

"You scared me," I tell him as I pull my ear buds out and hit pause on the playlist on my cell phone.

I can't work without music. I prefer it blaring over the sound system in the corner, but when I'm up here in the middle of the night, that's not exactly possible.

His intense blue eyes watch me carefully as a wide smile graces his full lips.

"Sorry, I didn't mean to..." His gaze shifts, and his apology is lost. "Are these yours?"

I feel the blush colour my cheeks – I don't make it a habit of showing people my work and he's still no exception to the rule.

Even Lucy, my best friend since we were in nappies, has never seen the entire collection of my work. I've shown her only two pieces, one of which she begged for until she wore me down and I agreed.

That particular piece sits proudly on the wall in the entry to her and Emmett's house, with a pinky promise from her that she'll never spill the beans on where she got it.

Rylan has never seen anything more from me than a doodle on a napkin and the 'safe' paintings my mum and dad have on their walls.

"Yeah... they're mine. I thought you'd be sleeping... I didn't mean to wake you. Do you want to go back to bed?"

"You didn't wake me," he murmurs as he slowly walks past me, his eyes studying one canvas before moving onto the next, ignoring my question about returning to the safety of my sheets.

I normally don't paint when he's here, but ever since he came home broken, I haven't slept much at all.

It was a rookie error on my behalf – leaving myself exposed this way, and even though I don't want to hide all of this from him forever, I'm not mentally prepared to have him in here right now.

This room is filled with my work and as he slowly takes appraisal of each piece, it's almost as though he's stripping me bare of an item of clothing.

These are my inner most thoughts and feelings – some of the images on these canvases are so raw and real they take me right back to the specific moment in time and the feelings hit me with such force it can literally knock me backwards.

That's why I keep it all up here, in the large attic, with a locked door.

The light provided from the huge skylights makes it the perfect place for me to paint –it's my happy place. But right now it feels more like a prison cell I can't escape.

Rylan's gently flicking through the stack of canvases against the wall now.

I suck in a ragged breath because I know exactly what he's seeing.

I haven't laid eyes on those paintings in close to two years, but each and every one of them is burned into my memory for all eternity.

Those are some of the hardest hitting works of art I've ever created.

I'm paralysed, almost gasping for air as I wait for him to question me on them, for him to ask things I can't answer.

But he doesn't.

When he reaches the last one, he rubs forcefully with the ball of his hand at a spot on his chest and glances around at the collection I have displayed on the far wall.

The relief I feel almost brings me to my knees.

These I can talk about, mainly because they make little to no sense to me.

He turns to face me for the first time in what feels like an eternity. He raises a dark brow at me. "What's with all the flowers?"

I shrug. "I'm not sure to be honest... I just started painting them one day, and I've never stopped."

"I like them," he whispers, his voice thick with an emotion I can't place.

"Thank you."

I don't tell him about the dream or *vision*, if you want to call it that, that I had a few years ago.

I don't tell him about the fields of daisies that everything important to me, including he himself was in.

I don't tell him that as soon as I was allowed home, I was back in front of a canvas, painting daisy after daisy, with no real idea why they were so important.

I can't tell him all of that. If I do, he'll have questions, and I'll end up telling him that he was there in my dreams – that I've been picturing him in my mind for nearly four years.

I'm still not quite ready for that revelation yet.

He strolls back over to me, leaving the other half of the room and the work in it safe from his intense stare.

There's a lot of memories over there too and a pair of blue eyes he was bound to recognise as his own, but I don't feel relief knowing he didn't see that particular painting, instead I still feel stripped bare as though he's already seen everything.

If there's one thing I've learnt about him in these past two months, it's that he misses nothing.

His mind is sharp, his eyes are focused, and his soul is curious.

He sees *everything*, even the things I don't say or show... he sees them too.

"Can we go for a walk?"

I'm surprised by his request, given that it's after midnight, but I'd give just about anything to be out of this room right now, so I nod eagerly, and when he holds out his hand to me, I take it.

Chapter Twenty

Rylan

We've walked for four blocks in total silence.

It's just us and the moonlight – much like it was after our very first date.

It's ironic really, that we've found ourselves out here again, only this time we're so far from strangers it's almost laughable.

She might not know everything there is to know about me yet, but right now, in this moment, I feel like I've seen every part of her soul.

Of course, I knew Violet painted.

I also knew she liked to keep her work to herself.

I've been dying to see even a glimpse of the magic she creates behind that door, but nothing could have possibly prepared me for what I saw tonight.

I'm under no illusion that me viewing her work was anything other than terrifying for her, but I had to do it.

There's this invisible barrier between us that's growing higher with each passing day we don't talk about our secrets.

On her side, it's her heart, her scars, her insecurities, and who knows what else.

On mine, it's the secret I'm keeping from her, it's my grief, my anger and my pain.

But that's about to change. Right now.

"There's something I need to tell you."

Her grip on my hand tightens and I feel terrible for my choice of wording.

I can't even imagine the things that might be going through her head right now, but instead of addressing all the things that I'm not holding back, I'm just going to come out with the thing that I *have* kept from her.

"You know our blind date?" I question her, and I see her nod out of the corner of my eye. "I didn't realise right away... but that wasn't the first time I'd ever seen you."

She stops walking and pulls me to a stop with her.

I'm expecting questions, confusion, and disbelief maybe... what I'm not expecting is for her to whisper the two words she does.

"I know."

She's looking down at her feet and I don't like it. Violet is the embodiment of the saying 'eyes are the windows to the soul'. Her eyes can conceal nothing, and I need to see them right now so I know we're okay.

I reach for her chin and tip it up so she can't hide from me any longer.

"You remember me?" I murmur. "From outside your hospital room?"

She nods, and I see her eyes begin to well up. "I recognised you the minute I saw you."

Suddenly it all makes sense. The panic attack she had on our first date – it was because she recognised me as the man from outside her window.

"Why didn't you say anything?"

She shrugs and the tears start to fall. "Why didn't *you*?"

I know what she means, and she's right – her reasons for not speaking up are probably the same as mine have been.

I don't know how I'm supposed to explain to her that she was a lifeline for me. That seeing her wake up gave me hope that maybe everything in the world wasn't so bad after all.

I've never told her about my sister, but I know I need to tell her now.

I want a life with Violet, and you can't build a life upon a mountain of secrets.

"You looked so lost," she whispers into the darkness.

"I've never been as lost as I was in those hours, Violet, and for some reason, *you* stopped me from falling apart."

"I don't understand..."

"I'm not sure I do either." I shake my head as I try to make sense of something that truly can't be explained.

"I didn't just happen to pass by your room, I'd been watching you for a while."

Confusion is written all over her face, and I don't blame her.

"I was in the ICU for...." My voice cracks, and I suck in a deep breath in an attempt to regain my composure. "For my sister."

She squeezes my hand again and rubs her thumb gently up and down the side of mine.

The small contact and comfort she gives me is enough for me to find the strength to go on.

"Her name was Daisy, and she died... there was a car crash... she fell asleep at the wheel after a twelve-hour shift and ran herself off the road."

Violet gasps and her hand flies up to cover her mouth. "Oh my God. I'm so sorry, Rylan, you never told me..."

"And then I saw you lying there and I couldn't stay away. My sister was dead, and I was drawn to you, I *needed* you to wake up and be okay. I had no idea what was wrong with you, but I could feel your struggle, Violet, and the moment you woke up and looked at me... I guess I felt hope again."

"I've never seen a person look the way you looked." Her voice sounds like sandpaper.

"You were the light for me, I was surrounded by darkness and *you* were what helped me see through it."

It feels like a huge weight has lifted off my shoulders. I've told Violet my truths, my secrets... and she's not mad at me for keeping it from her... she's still here and she loves me.

"I saw it in your eyes tonight – that same look."

I swallow the lump in my throat. "One of the nurses... she talked about Daisy today. It all hit me again... and then I came home to you, and you saved me, just like that first time."

"You saved me too, Rylan..." She goes to say something further, but I see the moment she catches herself. "Seeing you there, it did the same thing for me. You gave me hope too."

There's more – I can tell that she's holding something back from me, what, I have no idea, but I have a feeling that it's vitally important and I'm suddenly desperate to know.

"I need you to talk to me, Violet, please." I grasp her other hand in mine and tug her close. I know I'm begging, but I don't care – this is a pivotal moment for us, I've never felt a sense of urgency like I do here and now.

Her expression flickers between brave and ready, to frightened and wary.

She opens her mouth to speak, *finally,* and I brace myself for whatever it is she's about to tell me, but right at that moment, my cell phone rings in my pocket.

I drop my head forward in defeat, resting my forehead against hers.

It's my emergency ringtone and I know what that means – one of my patients is in labour.

I'm needed there, but I know on a deep level that I'm needed here just as much, if not more.

"You'd better get that."

She's looking down at my pocket as I stand unmoving.

I'm terrified that if I let this moment slip by right now that I'll never get it back.

She must sense my fear because she pulls her head back and looks at me, *really* looks at me.

"We can talk when you get back."

"You promise?" My voice is gruff and unsure, but I know I don't have another option.

I can't leave my patient and we both know it.

She pushes up to her tippy toes and kisses the side of my mouth. "Answer the damn phone, Rylan; you'll wake up all the neighbours."

She looks different; her face is serene – peaceful, as though maybe she's come to accept something in the same way I have.

She's also right; if I leave this phone ringing much longer there's going to be trouble.

I take the call and as I suspected I'm needed in the delivery ward immediately.

There's no time for any more talking, but as I back out of the driveway I see Violet in the window. She blows me a kiss and I fall even deeper in love with her.

I know in that instant that it doesn't matter what she tells me, I know it's only going to make me love her more.

***

I snap my gloves into place as I use my back to push open the door of the delivery suite.

"How are we doing in here, Luce?"

"Oh, thank God you're here," Emmett calls from his spot next to the bed.

Lucy has his hand in a death grip and I almost laugh – almost. If there's one thing I know, it's that women in labour do not tend to take jokes well.

I grab her chart from the maternity nurse and flick through the notes.

"Seriously, man, you gotta give her something, she's gone crazy."

"She's in labour, Emmett," I reply calmly at the same moment that Lucy screams at him.

"I'm in freakin' labour, you big dumb idiot!"

I hear Kristie, the nurse, try to muffle a laugh and I make the mistake of meeting her eyes.

I'm doing my best, I really am, but the look on Emmett's face right now is priceless.

"You had better not be laughing at me, Rylan Wilder, or so help me God… urrrrgggggghhhhhhhhh." Another contraction cuts off her threat.

"We're getting close now, Lucy."

I glance at my watch and make note of the time.

"How about I promise no more laughing, Emmett promises no more being a big dumb idiot, and we get that baby out of there, alright?"

She looks up at me for the first time and I see that she's all bark and no bite.

Lucy looks terrified.

"You've got this, I'm right here," I reassure her.

Emmett wipes a cool flannel across her face, and I can see that despite his wife's anger towards him, he is in fact doing a great job.

"I'm scared," she whispers.

"You can do this, baby, I'm right here with you." He kisses her forehead and I smile.

These two really are great together. They're going to make incredible parents.

"I want Violet." Lucy whimpers as another contraction builds. "Oh my God!" she cries as it hits full force. "I want Violet right now!"

Chapter Twenty-One

Violet

I race down the corridor that leads to the maternity wing of the hospital.

The baby that Rylan is delivering right now isn't just *any* baby, it's Lucy and Emmett's baby, and even though I was never planning to be in the delivery room with her – she needs me.

The fact that it was Emmett who called me and not Rylan, makes me think that perhaps I might be too late anyway, but I still run as fast as I can.

Lucy has been there for me through more than any friend should have to over the years. She's seen the absolute worst in me, and this might be the only chance I get to return the favour.

I approach the nurse's station panting for breath. "I'm looking for Lucy Hale," I say, far too loud and much too fast.

She points down the hall. "Room fourteen, Violet."

I yell my thanks over my shoulder as I take off running again. I'm pretty sure that not just anybody is allowed in here, so dating the obstetrician must have its perks.

I reach the numbered door and I can't hear anything, no screaming, no heavy breathing... *nothing...*

"Hello?"

I tap lightly on the door and I hear Lucy's voice call out to me.

"Come on in, Aunt Violet."

I slowly push open the door in wonder.

I know I'm not technically the baby's aunt, and that one day when August stops being so self-involved and settles down, or when Charlie grows up and stops serial dating – I might get some nieces and nephews that *are* related by blood, but the little bundle that I can see wrapped up in my best friend's arms – the sister I chose, will always be my family.

"Oh my God." I breathe the words.

I don't want to make even a sound and risk disrupting this moment of perfection.

Emmett is sitting on the side of the bed, right next to Lucy, and they're the most beautiful little family I've ever seen.

"You're only ten minutes too late."

I don't even have to look up to see who that voice belongs to. I would know it anywhere.

"It looks like you had it covered without me," I reply softly, my eyes still solely focused on the tiny baby in my best friend's arms.

"She's beautiful, huh?" Lucy catches my eye. She looks exhausted, but I've never seen her happier or more content than she looks right now.

"*She*?"

"You bet." Emmett nods. "My little princess." It's clear to see that this little girl already has her daddy securely wrapped around her finger.

"Her name is Harper Violet Hale," Lucy tells me. "We named her after her godmother." And with that statement I feel the tears start to fall.

***

"Did you know I was born in this hospital?"

I haven't turned to check he's there, but I don't need to, I know he followed me out here.

"You were?" he replies after a moment of silence.

I've been here for hours, watching my best friend be a mother, and I've literally never seen a sight more perfect. It fills me with warmth and cuts me deep in the very same breath.

Lucy deserves *every* ounce of happiness that little girl will bring her, but according to fate, I won't be afforded the same sense of joy.

I nod at him.

The silence stretches between us and I know he's waiting for me to speak.

"You were right earlier; there *is* something I need to tell you," I whisper, my voice shaky.

He moves closer to me and I take a minute to marvel at the feel of his warmth against my arm. He's such an amazing man – the fact he just ensured that my goddaughter made it into the world safe and healthy is an absolute testament to that. Knowing how special he really is just makes me all the more afraid I might lose him.

He's shared his most tightly kept secret with me tonight, and I owe him the same in return – it's time he knew everything about me, the same way I know him.

It can't have been easy for him to talk about his sister, but he did it. For me – for *us*.

His life reads like some type of sad story.

I might have experienced a lot, but he's been through his own brand of heartbreak too and I think that maybe he needs me as much as I need him.

I'm scared like I've never been scared before. It seems to be a reoccurring theme where Rylan is concerned. Maybe this is what being in love is like. Maybe I'll always be terrified about what will happen next.

"Tell me."

His hand reaches for mine and I take it gladly.

We're standing side by side, me watching Lucy, Emmett and baby Harper, and him watching me.

I don't know where I should even begin when it comes to telling this tale, but I figure the beginning is as good of a place as any.

"They tell me I died in this hospital too."

I hear his sharp intake of breath as the words hang in the air between us.

Chapter Twenty-Two

Rylan

"Come with me, there's something I need to show you."

She takes my hand and leads me towards the stairs, right up to the room where she paints.

I'm surprised by this, I wasn't expecting to be allowed back in here again anytime soon after my last intrusion, let alone welcomed with a personal escort, but after what she told me at the hospital I should have known that all bets were off.

She pauses outside the door and looks warily back over her shoulder at me.

"It'll be easier to explain if I show you as well as tell you."

I nod, even though I don't really understand where she's going with this. It doesn't matter, because I do know one thing – that wherever she's going, I'm going there too.

She rests her hand on the door handle and takes a deep, steadying breath.

I can feel the fear and insecurity radiating from her, but I don't say a word. I know she needs to work through this – whatever this is – for herself, and for us.

She eventually pushes the door open and I see why she's shaking like a leaf.

The display she's created is so confronting I can barely breathe.

I understand now exactly why she's kept all this hidden. These paintings say so much without actually having to say anything at all.

I'm gasping for air as my eyes start at the beginning, tracing over one work of art before moving onto the next.

She's so incredibly talented – the amount of emotion and passion that has gone into these is rivalled by nothing I've ever seen before.

"This is only a small part of my story. But it's the part that I think you need to hear the most."

My eyes dart around the room until I find her – standing by the very first painting in the big half circle she's made. It's one I've already seen, only a few short hours ago, but seeing it up on display makes it seem new again.

"I was twenty-one when my heart went into cardiac arrest less than a year before I had my transplant; they had to revive me twice. I was technically dead for a while there."

I look at the painting she's standing next to and I feel fear. Deep, irrational fear – I know I don't need to be afraid, because she's right here and she's okay... she's *alive*, but I can't look away and I can't seem to slow my heart rate.

"When I came back, I painted all of these."

She's never told me this part of her story and that scares me – I can't think of a reason she would have decided to keep it a secret.

I'm instantly filled with worry that maybe everything isn't as it seems – that perhaps there's still something threatening her life.

I love her – I love her more than I ever thought I could love another person, and the thought of a world where she doesn't exist just about brings me to my knees.

"Have you ever heard people say that their lives flashed before their eyes when they came close to death?" She's talking about something so life altering, yet her voice is serene, she looks like she's at peace.

I nod in acknowledgement – right now I can't speak.

"I saw it, Rylan, I saw my *whole* life. I saw my parents, my brother and sister, Lucy... they were all there."

She walks slowly past each painting as she speaks, and I feel like I'm right there on the verge of death with her. I feel like I've stepped into the so-called light and now *my* life is flashing before my eyes – because her life is my life now too. I'm not doing it without her.

My eyes follow her every movement, only leaving her face to look at each piece of art.

"But this was different than what they tell you in books or in the movies... I didn't see the life I'd already lived; I saw the life I should have had – the life that was mine if I survived..."

I don't understand what she means by that. I always assumed that before you died, if in fact your life did flash before your eyes, that you saw everything that had meant the most to you in the time you'd had.

"I guess it wasn't my time yet." She smiles, and I let out a breath I didn't realise I'd been holding. "Maybe one day, when it *is* my time, perhaps I'll see the past then..."

I don't even want to imagine the end of her life – I know it's been a very real possibility for her over the years, but I just can't allow my brain to go there.

"I think it was the only way to get me to come back, you know? To show me everything I should have had..."

"What did you see?" The words are out of my mouth without conscious thought, but I'm glad I said them. She's nearing the end of the paintings now, and there's only one left, but there's still so much left to tell – I can sense it.

The final piece is huge – it's covered with a sheet and I have a feeling that everything she's been keeping from me will be revealed once she lifts it.

I can already see so much of what she was looking at in those moments, the images, colours and scenes on the canvases in front of me are expressive and gut wrenching – but they're not why she brought me up here, I'm sure of it.

It's the painting under the sheet that I'm really here for.

She looks at me, her eyes pleading, for what, I'm not sure...

Understanding perhaps... forgiveness?

She tugs on the sheet and it reveals the painting behind it with a whoosh.

At first I don't understand. It's a set of eyes, deep blue eyes, and in the reflection of those eyes are daisies – fields of them, just like I saw earlier in her other paintings.

"You want to know what I saw, Rylan?"

I'm staring at the painting and I still don't understand what I'm looking at, but I think my brain is getting close to figuring it out.

"I saw *you*."

It's not until the word falls from her lips that I make the connection.

Those are my eyes.

My eyes are on a canvas that she painted four years ago – before I'd seen her for the first time, and I don't know what that means.

I can't fathom how any of this possibly makes sense.

"I saw *you*, Rylan... the last thing I saw was your eyes and the only thing I could hear in the darkness was your voice. You saved me."

"Me?" I stutter the word as I take a step closer. "I didn't know you, you didn't know me..."

"Yet you were outside my room all those months later... I don't know how to explain it, we'd *never* met... I don't know how it's possible..."

I tear my eyes away from the image and meet her gaze with what I'm sure is a look of utter confusion and wonder.

"But it *was* you, Rylan, I *do* know that."

***

"This might sound stupid, but it feels like I'm here for *you*," she whispers. "Maybe I survived because I hadn't found you yet... ever since I woke up, it's as though every moment has led me to this one."

I know exactly what she means.

The past three years never felt like they were going anywhere at all, but now that I'm here with her in my arms, it does seem like a journey.

It feels like there's a map imprinted on my heart, and every single road leads to her.

If it weren't for my sister's accident I never would have laid eyes on Violet. I never would have moved into Daisy's house and got a job at the hospital she worked in. I never would have met Emmett or Lucy, and I wouldn't have been set up on that first date with Violet.

I wouldn't be here now.

It devastates me to think that my sister dying had set something like this in motion – that without her leaving me, I never would have found the woman I love with everything I have.

There's a million thoughts flying through my head and I've got so many questions, but one thing seems to stand out among the rest.

Daisy... it was Daisy that brought us together.

I stroke Violet's hair before placing a tender kiss to her forehead.

We're out under the stars – in the place that's become ours.

Bear's here with us, and nothing has ever felt more right.

Even though I'm missing so much, I somehow feel complete.

I have everything I need right here, it's not everything I want from my life, but I know for certain that it *is* all I'll ever need.

I glance down at Violet and she's staring up at the dark vastness with a look of total wonder on her face. They're the very same stars we look at most nights, but each time she searches that sky it's like she's seeing it all for the very first time.

I've often found myself wondering what she sees through those eyes of hers.

She doesn't perceive things like the rest of us do. I know she has fears and worries, I know that she has more insecurities than most, but she has a sense of peace that surrounds her... it *envelops* her.

She sees the good in *everything* and that good is reflected back to her, almost as though she's absorbing it into her soul.

I'd give almost anything to look at the world through her eyes, even just for five minutes. I bet there's no one on earth that sees those stars the way she does.

"Rylan?" she whispers into the cool night air.

"Yeah?"

"What do you think it means?"

She's apprehensive about my answer. I can see her teeth worrying her bottom lip the way she always does when she's nervous.

I'm not sure I have an answer for her. When it comes to things like fate and destiny, I've never been a big believer, but there's no other way to explain this. I brought her back from the brink of death and in turn, she saved me in my darkest hour.

There's credit due to something or someone for that, but I don't have any idea where to begin with my thank yous.

I also don't know how to answer the woman I love.

I turn and push up onto my elbow so I'm leaning over her. "I think it means we're exactly where we're meant to be."

"You and me?" She whispers the words in a voice so uncertain it threatens to break my heart.

"You and me... *Us*... maybe it's as simple as the fact that we we're meant to put each other back together again."

Chapter Twenty-Three

Violet

"That's it… that's the whole story." My voice has wound up being so quiet I'm not sure she will have caught everything I said, but when I look up it's obvious she understands exactly what I've told her.

I didn't come over here with the intention to spill my guts to Lucy like this, but when beautiful little Harper fell asleep in my arms, the story had just flowed from me for some reason.

I'm still not entirely sure why I never told Lucy about what happened to me – and as strange as it was to have a secret from her all these years, in a way I'm glad I did.

Auggie might have known this whole time, but it was all just a dream until Rylan turned up. Now that he's here and we're together, it really has developed into one hell of a story.

"So I can't take credit for you two after all?" She pouts, and I laugh.

Of course *that* would be her first response.

Luce is so proud of herself for setting us up; her and Emmett haven't stopped gloating about it since we became an official couple.

I am incredibly grateful to them both, and I don't want to burst her bubble, but I think she was just a pawn in something much bigger than any of us.

"I hate to break it to you, but I think I saw him first."

I'm surprised she isn't bombarding me with questions and demanding answers, but right now she seems to just be absorbing everything I've told her.

I can't blame her for needing a minute to process, it's taken me a long time to get my head around, and I'm the one who experienced it.

I wouldn't fault Lucy if she didn't believe me at all – it's a pretty surreal and farfetched tale, but she always has been a bit more spiritual than me, so she's likely to deem the whole thing as destiny.

"I think I felt it, you know? The first moment I met him, it was *you* that popped into my head. In my brain at least, the two of you have always been connected."

It makes me happy that she thinks of the two of us like that.

I've thought a lot about it lately – how we're all intertwined with one another's stories. Lucy and I, Lucy and Emmett, Rylan and I, Emmett and Rylan, Emmett and I... all three of these people are responsible in their own way for saving my life – for keeping me alive both emotionally and physically.

I may have been dealt a really shitty health hand over the years, but I've been handed an absolute winning combination when it comes to company, love and relationships, and if I think about it, I'm not sure I'd trade one for the other.

I'd rather experience the struggles I have and be around these incredible people, than have a perfect bill of health with no one of any significance to share it with.

"I'm *so* glad you found him, Letty – even if it wasn't because of my match making skills – you deserve to be happy."

I've got goose bumps on my arms and legs still – it happens every time I think about what I saw in my vision.

"You know, I pictured him in my sleep every night for years... but I don't have to dream anymore, Luce, I can just roll over and he's there. It's surreal – my whole life feels like a dream now."

"That must be the *weirdest* thing."

"I have to keep convincing myself that it *is* real..."

"It's real." She smiles sadly at me and I know it's because she understands why I'm always waiting for it all to go wrong – that's the way it's been my whole life. "He's not going anywhere, I've seen the way he looks at you – he might be willing to fight for you even harder than I have."

I can't imagine anyone other than my mum and dad fighting harder for me than Lucy has, but when I picture Rylan in my mind, I can't help but consider that maybe he might be the strongest fighter of all.

***

Rylan is still out in the garage working with Emmett – he's helping him build a set of shelves for Harper's room and while they're out there throwing around their testosterone and man skills, I'm getting my baby fix.

"She's seriously *so* cute, how do you get anything done? I just want to stare at her all day." I swoon.

"Why do you think my washing pile is so huge?" Lucy grumbles half-heartedly.

She's not joking either – I do at least two loads every time I come over and it barely makes a dent in the huge mountain.

Harper is still sleeping peacefully in my arms and she's just so unbelievably beautiful. It's hard to believe she's real – until she's exercising the strong set of lungs she's got on her anyway.

I run my finger lightly over her cheek and smile at her total perfection.

I hear the click of a camera. I look up and Lucy is smiling at the picture she's just captured of me and her little girl.

I scowl at her, photos have never really been my favourite thing, but I don't bother complaining, it would only fall on deaf ears.

"It suits you, Letty." She looks between her daughter and me.

A lump forms in my throat the instant the words leave her mouth and I have to fight to swallow it down.

I don't know why I'm getting so emotional about it, but all of a sudden, I can feel tears forming in the corner of my eyes.

The fact that I'll never have my own baby isn't a new revelation; in fact, it's something I've thought about a lot over the years. Especially lately, after I've spent time with my goddaughter – it's a topic that's been pretty front and centre in my mind.

It's not that I want a baby right now, because I don't – not yet... but one day I would have loved to be a mother.

I know there are other options like adoption and surrogacy, but I also realise that those are easy things to talk about, but unfortunately not so easy to make happen. They're expensive and time consuming, and even then, there's no guarantee.

"I'm not sure it's on the cards for me."

"You *saw* a baby, Vi."

"That doesn't mean it'll happen."

I'm aware that I saw Rylan, and I got him – but that doesn't mean this will work the same way.

A baby is in no way promised to me because of something I conjured up in my mind in a near-death experience.

I've been given *so* much; I know it's not fair of me to expect anything more. I already owe so much more than I'm owed in return.

"Violet," says the voice I'd recognise even in my sleep.

I had no idea Rylan was listening to us, so when he speaks it startles me.

He steps into the room and the sight of his intense stare on my face takes my breath away.

"If you want a baby, I'll do *anything* I can to make it a reality for us."

He crouches down next to me and wraps his arms around my body. It makes me feel safe and while he's right here, holding me close, I believe what he's telling me.

He rests his forehead against mine and glances down at the precious little girl in my arms.

"I can't promise you a baby, but I can promise you we'll try every option there is, if that's what you want, okay?"

I know he means it – babies and reproductive organs are literally his speciality, but I can't allow myself to get my hopes up where this is concerned.

"And if it doesn't happen?" My voice cracks.

"If it doesn't happen then we'll get through it *together*. I don't know how many times I have to say this before you'll believe me, but *you* are all I need."

I *do* believe him, but that doesn't mean I don't feel guilt or worry over it.

I know I'm enough for him, and he's enough for me too.

I do want a baby one day, I want one *so* badly, but deep down I know that *he's* enough.

We've got each other and that'll always be everything I need, but I can't help but wish that it wasn't another sacrifice he has to make because he's fallen in love with a broken woman.

Chapter Twenty-Four

Rylan

"Tell me about your sister."

Violet's lying on the couch, with her eyes closed and her head in my lap, and I honestly thought she'd nodded off.

I have a feeling she's been up all night painting while I slept because she's been totally exhausted all day.

"What do you want to know?" I ask as I twirl a strand of her hair around my finger.

"Anything," she breathes. "Just tell me *anything*."

I feel guilty for not being more open with her – ever since I told her about losing my sister we have talked about her, but it's been those types of conversations where you do a lot of talking but at the same time, say nothing at all.

Violet knows my sister's name and that she was a doctor... she knows that after she died I moved here and into her house.

I've told her about my dad passing away when I was a teenager and about my now elderly mother who suffered early onset dementia back home.

She doesn't know anything about who Daisy was as a person or the fact that she basically raised me at times. She doesn't know that we shared a mother, but not a father and that we were all each other had for a good portion of my life.

I want to tell her everything, I really do, but every time I try, the words get caught in my throat and pushed back down deep.

I know I should talk about her more – Daisy deserves to be remembered and not forgotten, and I know it's important to Violet too, so I put down the book I was reading, take a deep breath and start talking as best I can.

"I remember when I was eleven, Daisy would have been about twenty-one, it was my birthday, and my parents had promised me a skateboard. It was the only thing I wanted, and I was so excited to finally be getting one. Anyway, the day came, Dad was sick, and Mum was already beginning to forget things, and that's what happened to my skateboard – they forgot to get one for me." I'd put on a brave face and told them it didn't matter, but truthfully, I was devastated.

I know now that it's just a toy, and if I'd known at the time that only a year and a half later my father would be gone, and that my mother's mind would be taken from her not long after that, I doubt I would have cared about doing anything other than spending the day with the both of them.

That's the real kicker about hindsight.

"I'll never forget the look on Daisy's face when she realised what had happened. She disappeared for an hour and when she came back she had with her the same exact skateboard I'd pointed out in the store a few weeks before."

"She sounds like a good big sister," Violet murmurs, her eyes still shut.

"She was the best."

It hurts my heart that I have to say 'was' instead of 'is' – that I have no choice but to talk about her in past tense rather than present.

"It was a beautiful sunny day, and the four of us went down to the park so I could practise using it. Daisy stayed there with me all day, long after Mum and Dad headed back home. She wasn't too cool for her little brother, or too busy either. When she moved away she always made sure to come home for things like birthdays and holidays. She loved me the same way a mother loves her child – *unconditionally*."

"You miss her a lot." It's not a question, but a statement.

"Every single day."

Violet yawns and wiggles around to get more comfortable. "Tell me another story."

So I tell her the very next thing I can think of.

"She's the reason I went to med school."

"Yeah?" she answers sleepily.

"I got really good grades in high school, but I had no idea what I was going to do when it came time to leave. I went to visit Daisy once; she was working as a GP in a small town while she furthered her study. She was running late so I went into the clinic to wait for her.

A lady in the waiting room started talking to me. She went on and on about how much Daisy had helped improve the symptoms of her arthritis, but it wasn't just her Daisy had helped, it seemed that everyone in town had a problem my sister had looked at and done her best to fix. She was *helping* people – giving back to the world, and it just dawned on me that I wanted to do that too.

Daisy's always done that for me – lead by example. She never put any pressure on me to make a decision about my future; she never even suggested medicine as a potential field for me. Instead she just showed me the way.

I enrolled last minute, and I don't know how, but I got accepted, and as they say, *the rest is history*."

I realise I'm smiling as I talk about my sister. This is the first time I've associated her memory with any emotion other than despair and I'm shocked that I've managed it.

I look down at Violet, so I can share my achievement with her, but when my eyes land on her pretty face, it's obvious she's finally let sleep take her.

Her lips are parted, and her breathing is deep and steady.

She might not be able to hear me, but that doesn't mean I can't talk.

I tug the blanket off the back of the couch and drape it gently over her before telling her story after story – filling in her sleeping form about exactly who my sister was.

Chapter Twenty-Five

Violet

There's something I need to do – something I've been putting off for a long while now because it just seems too... *hard*.

I need to make contact with the family of my donor.

It's been four years now since they lost their loved one and I still know nothing about the person who in death, saved my life.

I don't know if it was a man or a woman, or if they were young or old.

I don't know how they died or if their organs were used to save anybody else.

I don't know what they did for a job or how many people they left behind.

I don't know a single thing about them, so I know it's time to reach out now.

The only option I have is a letter. I can give a letter to the hospital's transplant co-ordinator, who will pass it onto the family of my donor. It's up to them if they want to reply, or even read it at all, and even if I never hear back, at least I'll know I tried.

I don't know what I'm supposed to write – I don't know the right way to thank someone for the unbelievable gift I've been given.

I could ask Rylan for help, but he already does so much for me, and this feels like something I need to do on my own.

I started this journey a long time ago, and I need to finish this final chapter. Who knows what might happen after that – maybe sometime soon I'll be ready to close the book entirely.

I think about the selfless gesture that organ donation is.

I think about the people my donor left behind.

I think about the heart beating in my chest and how I owe my life to someone else.

Each thump of the borrowed organ is so important, so *significant* that suddenly I know exactly what I need to say.

I reach for a sheet of paper and a pen and write from deep inside my soul.

To the owner of my heart,

You don't know me, and I know you can't read this, but I still need to write it.

My name is Violet Miller, and four years ago, you saved my life.

If you hadn't have ticked that little box labelled 'donor', it's entirely possible I wouldn't be here right now, so for that I thank you – you chose to be selfless where you could have been selfish instead.

There's no possible way I could ever repay you, so instead I'll spend the rest of my life living, really living each moment as it was intended to be lived. I can't give you much, but I can do that – for both of us.

There's so many things I wish I could say to you, and it hurts me to know that I'll never get the chance.

I want you to know that I'm so, so sorry. I can't even begin to explain the guilt I carry with me every day, knowing that your life was given in exchange for mine.

Why am I here, and you're not?

I know that's a question I'll probably never get an answer to.

There's a lot of things in this world that make sense to me, but why I was spared when others were taken is something I'm not sure I'll ever understand.

I hope that whoever you left behind is managing as best they can. I may not have met you, but I don't need to have known you to understand the hole you left in the lives of those closest to you.

I've thought a lot lately about fate, and what happens when we die... I'm still not sure exactly what I believe, but I do think that there's some place good for those who deserve it, and I know that wherever that is, you're there.

I have so many questions about you, but I know it's not my place to ask. I don't expect your family or friends to give me those answers, they've given me enough already. I just hope they can find some peace knowing that I'm alive because of you.

Thank you for my life, I promise to live it.

Violet – The keeper of your heart.

Chapter Twenty-Six

Rylan

I knock lightly on the door to the small office I haven't set foot in for over four years.

I'm in such a different place now than I was back then, that it really doesn't look like the same room at all as I open the door.

The paintings on the walls are brighter now, the room doesn't feel like it's caving in around me anymore, and I notice the light streaming in through the window, rather than the dark shadows that light creates.

I'm a different person than I was.

I have Violet to thank for that.

The only constant between my life then and my life now, is *her*.

She was the light back then, and she's been that same light every day for the past year I've spent with her.

"Dr. Wilder." The middle-aged woman smiles at me.

She's a work colleague I don't see often – this hospital is a big place, but yet I don't think I'll ever forget her face.

She was my counsellor for a year. I may not have thought that we made one single inch of progress in that time, but given that I'm here now and I'm doing so much better, I have to admit that maybe it did help me in some small way.

"Rylan, please," I tell her as I take the seat she's indicating I should sit in.

This whole set up feels like I've been sent to the principal's office. I don't know why I'm here, but I have a feeling in the pit of my gut that it's serious.

"Rylan." She smiles at me.

I don't smile back; I can't seem to make the muscles in my cheeks work.

"You're probably wondering why I asked you in here."

"I am."

"I was wondering if we could talk about your sister for a minute."

I can't fathom for a second what she would possibly want to talk to me about in regards to my sister.

Daisy has been gone for a long time now.

As much as I'm confused by this topic, I'm also proud of myself for thinking of Daisy without the pain and heartache I've long since grown accustomed to.

I'm making progress – they might only be small steps, like contacting some of the people I let slip away during my grief, but for me, it feels like a huge leap I'm taking in the right direction.

I know I have Violet to thank for that too.

I still don't talk about Daisy a lot, and I haven't managed to put up or even share with Violet all our old photos yet, but it's progress, and my heart doesn't ache the same way when I think of her anymore.

I still miss her like crazy, and I think there will always be a little piece of me that's missing, but this is the most whole I've felt in a very long time.

"Rylan?" she asks, and I realise I never answered her.

"Sorry, sure, go ahead."

"Do you recall, when you began your employment here, that you were asked to fill out a few pages of questions?"

I know exactly what she's talking about.

The questionnaire is designed as a safe guard – a guide for the families and loved ones of the doctors and nurses that work in this hospital should anything ever happen to us.

I've seen what can happen in an emergency situation, a patient is brought in and their family has no idea what they would have wanted in terms of medical intervention.

When I started here, I answered questions about who I wanted notified if anything might happen to me, whether I'd want to be resuscitated or have my life artificially prolonged... if I agreed to have my organs harvested for donation or my body donated to science.

"I remember," I tell her.

"Do you also remember giving authority at the time of Daisy's death to honour all of the decisions she made on *her* form?"

My sister worked here too – she answered the same questions I did.

I nod, my throat feeling suddenly thick with emotion.

I can remember the moment as though it were only yesterday.

I signed that sheet of paper without a second thought – whatever Daisy wanted, that was what she got. She always knew better than me when it came to these kinds of things, but even if she didn't, I would never have gone against the wishes of my sister on the day of her death.

I still don't know what her final requests were, but I agreed to all of them without a moment's hesitation.

"I have a letter here for you... it's from a patient whom Daisy donated an organ to."

I don't even realise that I've been staring at the ground until I hear her words and my head snaps up.

"Daisy was a donor?"

She nods at me. "She donated to five deserving people."

I don't know why the possibility never occurred to me before now, but *of course* Daisy was a donor.

She was one of the most generous people I've ever met.

"No one told me," I whisper.

"Perhaps you didn't want to hear it?" she offers.

When Daisy was brought in, I couldn't bring myself to ask the extent of the damage caused by the crash, let alone if something like organ donation was a viable option, so instead I stuck my head in the sand and questioned nothing at all.

Much like I did my friends, I shut out any and all things Daisy for a long time, so there's a good chance someone did try to tell me, but I just wasn't willing to listen.

I don't know how I feel about the fact that there are five people out there in the world, each carrying around a little part of my sister, but I know that Daisy would have wanted it to be this way.

"You said there was a letter?" My voice is hoarse and scratchy.

She nods and hands it over to me. "I'll give you a minute alone."

I don't look up as she exits the room.

There's a thin envelope in my hands that feels like a heavy brick, and all of a sudden, I *have* to know what it says.

I tear the flap open and pull out the letter from inside.

My hands are shaking so badly it takes me a couple of attempts to read the first few lines, and when I do, the sheet of paper falls to the floor.

To the owner of my heart,

You don't know me, and I know you can't read this, but I still need to write it.

My name is Violet Miller, and four years ago, you saved my life...

Chapter Twenty-Seven

Violet

Even though we've unofficially been living together with Bear for what feels like forever, it's never felt more real than it does today. Rylan's not even here right now, but my home is so filled with him I can barely remember what it was like before he appeared in my life.

There's a whole pile of boxes stacked against the wall, and even though I'm expecting him home any time now to help me, I can't seem to stop myself from taking one down and starting to unpack it.

It's labelled 'photos' and I have to admit that it's got my curiosity piqued.

Rylan talks about his parents often and while I've seen a couple of pictures of his late father and his elderly mother, I'm still yet to see even one of his sister Daisy.

I know it's not for the fact that he doesn't want to show me, but that it just hurts him too much – he never fully dealt with his sister's death, but I think that these past few months he's finally starting to heal.

I glance at the clock again.

There's a sensation lurking around me like I'm doing something wrong, but I shove it aside. Rylan and I are in this life together – I know that nothing that lives in a box could possibly come between us.

I lift the lid and find a few albums, some frames and a couple of stacks of photos.

I shuffle through a few until I spot an envelope.

There's only two photos inside, I recognise one as Rylan's mum and dad when they were younger. I smile at the obvious love between them – his dad is looking at his mum the same way that Rylan looks at me.

This photo deserves to be in a frame, displayed proudly on the wall, so I sit it down on the table to tell Rylan when he gets home that we'll be doing exactly that with it.

I pull the other photo from the envelope at the same time as I hear the front door open.

I clutch my chest in shock, I can't believe what I'm seeing.

The image that has taken my breath away is of Rylan, he's about ten years younger here than he is now and he's *so* handsome, but it's not that – it's the woman next to him, who I now have no doubt is his sister, that's caused me to gasp aloud.

I *know* this woman, and the realisation of exactly who she is steals the last of my reservations about fate.

"Violet." Rylan's voice startles me.

I turn and look at him, and he's there, his eyes filled with what appears to be total disbelief.

We stand unmoving, staring at one another in wonder.

In my hand is the photo that's just completely blown my mind, and in his, he holds a sheet of paper that signifies the final piece of our puzzle clicking into place.

Epilogue

Violet

I hear someone clinking cutlery against glass, indicating that they want to make a speech and I spin around, looking for the speaker.

I recognise his voice a fraction of a second before my eyes land on his face, in all its smiling perfection.

The earth has circled the sun five times since he officially came into my life, yet every time I look into his startling blue eyes; it feels like the very first time.

"I'd like to make a toast." He smiles at me and my belly flips.

I don't know how he does that. He *still* has the power to turn my insides to mush, even after all these years.

"Thank you all for coming... there's two very special women I need to make mention of tonight, the first being my beautiful wife."

He smiles so wide at me that everybody else in the room follows suit, looking at me and smiling along with him.

I know I'm bright red, but I don't care, his words mean more to me than anybody else's and right now, he's *all* I can see.

"The art you're about to witness, she has been working on for literally her entire life. She has laid herself bare on those canvases, and for her to allow the whole world to see them is certainly no small feat."

He looks at me with such tenderness in his eyes I have to fight to hold his gaze rather than shy away from it.

"I can personally vouch for the rollercoaster of emotions that you'll experience when you walk through those doors... because trust me; some of those paintings have the power to bring you to your knees."

The skin on my arms has broken out into goosebumps now; all the individual little hairs are standing up on end. He's the only person close to me to see my collection in its entirety thus far, and I know he means every word he's saying.

Lucy reaches for my hand and grips it tightly in hers.

Her belly is round for the third time and her skin is positively glowing again, only this time it's not her bun she's cooking in her oven, it's *mine*.

I squeeze her hand back appreciatively; I'm so incredibly grateful for the selfless woman I get to call my best friend. She knows me as well as she knows herself, so she of all people understands exactly how nervous I am right now.

"Congratulations, gorgeous, I can't think of a single person who deserves this moment more than you do." Rylan lifts his flute of wine in my direction.

I hold back tears as I walk towards him and he wraps me in his strong, safe arms while everybody around us claps and cheers.

"Thank you," I murmur against his chest.

He kisses the top of my head and when I pull away, he tucks me into his side, his arm wrapping protectively around me, the same way it always has.

"But there's also one other woman I need to thank tonight."

I already know what he's going to say next, and just the mere thought of it has the first of what I'm sure will be many tears slipping down my face.

"My sister."

Everyone is watching him closely, intrigued by his words. He's always been the kind of man that commands the attention of a room, but I think we can all feel that this is something more.

"All of you already know that some years back, Violet's life was saved when she received a heart transplant... but there's one thing that some of you probably don't know, something that neither Violet or I knew when we first met either."

I think back to the moment when I decided that I undoubtedly believed in fate.

"A few years ago, Violet reached out to her donor's family, she wrote a beautiful, heartfelt letter expressing how grateful she was... and not long after, I *received* a letter. It was from a bright, incredible woman who told me that someone in my family had saved her life... it was only then that I realised *my* sister was her donor."

I hear a few gasps from the crowd.

He looks down at me now, his eyes glistening with unshed tears, but his expression bright and happy.

He's finally made peace with the tragedy that took his sister's life and in turn, gave me mine.

"My sister gave life to the woman who would later become the love of mine and I know it was her that brought the two of us together."

He kisses my head again, but I know this time it's for his benefit, not mine. He draws strength from being close to me, and he needs that strength right now as he talks about the possibility of my life coming to an end and as he relives the memory of his sister losing hers.

"Violet's told me about how she technically died once, when she was twenty-one years old… she told me about her heart going into cardiac arrest and about the woman who brought her back from the brink of death. But it wasn't until much later on that I knew without a shadow of a doubt that it was my sister Daisy that brought Violet and I together."

My mum, dad and brother are eyeing me curiously now, but Auggie, she just looks totally serene – like maybe she already knows what's coming.

He turns so he's speaking directly to my family. "My sister was a cardiologist… you knew her actually… she would have introduced herself as Dr. White – she was the woman who saved Violet's life that day."

I can hear my mum sobbing now as the weight of what he's saying presses down on all of us. We chose to save that final piece of information for this exact moment and I'm glad we did. Daisy's memory deserves this honour.

The fact that Dr. White – the woman who brought me back to life and then treated me for the months that followed afterwards – is not only his sister, but also my donor, still blows my mind each and every time I think about it.

"So…" he takes a deep steadying breath, "I just wanted to thank her, because it takes an incredible woman to not only save lives *in* life, but also in death."

He raises his glass to the sky now.

"To Daisy, *thank you*, even though you're gone, you've somehow managed to do what you've always done – you gave me a life worth living."

The group surrounding us erupts into applause and I feel myself being pulled into embrace after embrace.

Tears are flowing freely down my face, along with everyone else in the room.

I glance up at the daisy chain I painted on the welcome banner and smile. They're the same ones from my vision, the ones I never really understood until that final connection between Rylan and I was made.

The daisies are for *Daisy*.

I've dreamt about this moment for so long – the moment where I'm brave enough to share my work with the world, and also where we can pay tribute to the woman who saved my life on more than one occasion, and now it's *finally* here.

I'm eventually released by my friends and family, and right on cue the doors are opened to allow everyone into the gallery to witness my exhibition for the very first time.

I'm terrified of what people will think, but with Rylan looking at me like I'm *everything,* I know that I have what it takes to be exactly that in this world.

I run my fingertip gently over the cover of the booklet in my hand.

The two words looking back at me, much like the beating organ in my chest, are as much hers as they are mine.

It's the introduction to my life's work, to everything I've ever kept hidden, and it's simply titled *'My Heart'*.

The end

"Every new beginning comes from some other beginnings end."
-Seneca

Other Titles

Love like Yours Series
Rushed – Book 1
Pierced – Book 2
Hunted – Book 3
Chased – Book 4

Rock Games Novels
Paper, Scissors, Rock: Vol. 1
Hide and Seek: Vol. 2

My Heart Duet
My Heart Needs
My Heart Wants

Acknowledgements

Thank you to everyone that has taken a chance on this duet – it's been a really nervous time for me, as these two books are so different from anything I've ever written before, so to every reader, new or old, thanks so much for reading My Heart Needs and continuing on to My Heart Wants to see the rest of Violet's journey.

To my editor and readers and those of you part of my process to get my books published, thanks so much, I appreciate everything you do for me.

Once again I'd like to acknowledge the journey of those living with conditions like Violet's, you all are such an inspiration and I hope I've done this story justice.

Thank you all for the support!

About the Author

NICOLE S. GOODIN is a romance author and mother of two from Taranaki in the North Island of New Zealand.

In mid-2015, she started to write about a group of characters who wouldn't get out of her head. Her first book, Rushed, was published in mid-2016.

Nicole enjoys long walks on the beach, pillow fights and braiding her friends' hair. She dislikes clichés, talking about herself in the third person, and people who don't understand her sense of humour.

Please feel free to contact her either via her website, email, Instagram, Twitter or on her Facebook page, she would love to hear your feedback. If you're feeling really game, you can even sign up for her newsletter.

Visit www.nicolegoodinauthor.com for more information.